IR

Irish Life and Lore

SÉAMAS Ó CATHÁIN

THE MERCIER PRESS
CORK

The Mercier Press Limited
Cork

ISBN 978 1 78117 914 7

Pour Sorcha et Monique

Transferred to Digital Print-on-Demand in 2024

Contents

The Wild Rapparee   7

Hags and Hares   22

The Day of the Horse   33

Cats   45

First and Last   53

Dead and Buried   65

Begging their Bit   76

Tea   89

Still Going Strong   101

Sláinte!   112

Notes   123

Acknowledgements

I wish to thank the Head of the Department of Irish Folklore, University College, Dublin for permission to publish material drawn from the folklore manuscript collection lodged there and the Folklore of Ireland Society for permission to quote extracts from material first published in its journal, *Béaloideas*.

To the men and women who told the stories that enliven these pages and to their friends, the collectors, whose privilege it was to gather this material from them, I also wish to extend my best thanks. *Faraor géar, tá cuid mhaith acu seo ar shlí na fírinne cheana féin. Go ndéana Dia trócaire orthu.*

Helsinki 1982

The Wild Rapparee

The hunted man has for ages received the more or less uninquiring sympathy of the Irish people. In Irish he used to be called *Tóraí*, later anglicised Tory, which literally means 'the hunted one' and, of course, he was also called the rapparee, a word whose derivation from the Irish *ropaire* (itself a loan-word from the English 'robber') somehow throws a less endearing light on his character. Whatever about that, in Ireland, ordinary people always seem to have had a regard for the man who, against mighty odds, still held himself independent of the law, which he despised, and who, while he robbed the rich, had an ever open hand for the poor and the oppressed. Without a doubt, very few of the Irish rapparees could ever have run the course they did had they not fully enjoyed the sympathy of the masses.

It is no surprise, therefore, that the dominating image of the wild rapparee is the romantic one — he is an outlaw engaged in a lonely and courageous battle against foreign oppression and he is a swashbuckling hero, gallant and full of fight, but for all his cleverness and guile, nevertheless destined to end his days at the end of a rope or to die a violent death in some other way, frequently as a result of being treacherously and shamefully betrayed by his own people.

The seventeenth century saw its fair share of these men, sad leftovers from the Irish wars, who roved the country in bands and continued to worry and harry the English many years after Aughrim and the Boyne. Story's *Continuation of the History of the Wars in Ireland* (published in 1693) gives the following account of them:

'These men knew the country, nay, all the secret corners, woods and bogs; keeping a constant correspondence with one another, and also with the army, who furnished them with all necessaries, especially ammunition. When they had any project on foot, their method was not to appear in a body, for then they would have been discovered; and not only so, but carriages and several other things had been wanting which every one knows that is acquainted with this trade: their way was, therefore, to make a private appointment to meet at such a pass or wood, precisely at such a time o' th' night or day as it stood with their conveniency; and though you could not see a man over night, yet exactly at their hour you might find three or four hundred, more or less, as they had occasion, all well armed, and ready for what design they had formerly projected; but if they happened to be discovered or overpowered, they presently dispersed, having before-hand appointed another place of rendezvous, ten or twelve miles (it may be) from the place they were at; by which means our men could never fix any close engagement upon them during the winter; so that if they could have held out another year, the *Rapparees* would have continued still very prejudicial to our army, as well by killing our men privately, as stealing our horses and intercepting our provisons. But after all, lest the next age may not be of the same humour with this, and the name of a *Rapparee* may possibly be thought a finer thing than it really is, I do assure you that in my stile they never can be reputed other than Tories, Robbers, Thieves, and Bog-trotters.'[1]

An Impartial History of the Affairs of Ireland during the last Ten Years, published in 1691, contains the following description of an attack by the English on a party of rapparees near Mountmellick:

'After some resistance, they killed thirty-nine, and took four, whom they hanged without any further ceremony. The rest escaped to the bogs, and in a moment all disappeared, which may seem strange to those that have not seen it, but something of this kind I have seen myself: and those of this party assured me that, after the action was over, some of them, looking about amongst the dead, found one *Dun,* a sergeant of the enemies, who was lying like an otter, all under water, in a running brook (except the top of his nose and his mouth); they brought him out, and altho' he proffer'd Forty shillings in English money to save his life (a great ransom, as he believed), yet he was one of the four that was hanged. When the rapparees have no mind to shew themselves upon the bogs, they commonly sink down between two or three little hills, grown over with long grass, so that you may as soon find a hair as one of them. They conceal their arms thus: they take off the lock, and put it in their pocket, or hide it in some dry place; they stop the mussle close with a cork, and the tutch-hole with a small quill, and then throw the piece itself into a running water or a pond. You may see a hundred of them without arms, who look like the poorest humblest slaves in the world, and you may search till you are weary before you find one gun; but yet when they have a mind to do mischief, they can all be ready in an hour's warning, for every one knows where to go and fetch his own arms, though you do not.'[2]

One of the most famous of the breed of Northern rapparees was Redmond O'Hanlon who dubbed himself 'Chief Ranger of the Mountains, Surveyor General of the High Roads, Lord Examiner of all Passengers and High Protector of his Benefactors and Contributors'. His exploits were reported and recorded far and wide, including such places as the French gazettes of the time, which invariably styled him 'Count O'Hanlon' — a title denoting that he was of gentle blood. Be that as it may, when he appeared publicly he always observed a sort of state befitting his exalted position, wearing rich apparel and, when mounted, riding a well-bred charger. From his haunts in the Fews above Newry, he lorded it over Counties Armagh, Down, Monaghan and Louth and within those territories no one without a very strong escort dared to travel unless they had a pass from him. Like all true rapparees, he also seemed to have perfected the art of being in two places at once, a circumstance which led one writer to comment:

'If ever a mere mortal was possessed of the gift of ubiquity, Redmond O'Hanlon was, without any manner of question, the man. A bird was not to be put in comparison with him; for what bird was ever known that could be in more places at a time than two? Redmond O'Hanlon was in two dozen. He was everywhere, in fact, for those whom he looked for, and nowhere for those who looked for him. That was the most curious thing about Redmond; there was plenty of him where he could be spared, and the greatest possible scarcity where he was wanted. Go whither you would, to Cape Clear, or the Giant's Causeway, to Dingle or Downpatrick, to Waterford or Westport, you were as sure to meet Redmond O'Hanlon, if you had no particular wish for it, as you were to miss him if you had. The result of such an encounter it is needless to enlarge on. Suffice it to say that your watch went — faster than you had ever known it to do; that your gold was taken without weighing, and your jewels, if you had any. . . removed to safer custody than your own had proved to be. All this, however, was obviated if you were fortunate enough to be able to produce a 'pass' bearing O'Hanlon's signature and certifying the holder of it to be a person travelling under his protection. Such passes were to be obtained by the payment of a certain yearly tribute to the grantor, not very extravagant in amount; and the wayfarer who carried with him a safe conduct of this sort, had no confiscations to fear on the road, though he should ride with money-bags, instead of pistols, at his saddle-bows, and parade his gold repeater and diamond ring in the face of every strange horseman he met with.'[3]

Redmond thrived on his reputation as the greatest rogue in Ireland but for all that he was not invincible, as one cunning merchant who had placed himself under his protection but had apparently failed to renew his annual pass, managed to prove. The merchant, held at gun-point, was able to show that the pass which Redmond had believed to have expired was, in fact, still valid, for, on the date of the previous renewal — the merchant's birthday as it happened — Redmond had agreed to the merchant's request to have the term of his pass run from birthday to birthday, rather than quoting the actual date. The merchant's birthday fell on the 29th of February and thus occurred only once every four years which meant that he had fooled Redmond into granting him four years' protection for the price of one.[4]

Michael J. Murphy from Dromintee in County Armagh, and therefore a native of the border country where Redmond O'Hanlon once held sway, has spent a good many years collecting folklore for the former Irish Folklore Commission and for the Department of Irish Folklore at University College, Dublin in whose service he has ranged all over the north of Ireland and parts of the west of Ireland too, seeking out storytellers and tradition bearers of all kinds. One of the best of these storytellers he found on his own doorstep, in Ravensdale, County Louth, and from this man, James Loughran, he recorded, in 1962, a story describing how a highwayman, even a highwayman as formidable as our Redmond, could be outwitted by falling victim to his own greed:

'There was a merchant here in Dundalk, a shop-

11

keeper, and he had money to get off a man in Newry and he could get no one to take it to him. They were all afraid of this Redmond O'Hanlon. And this wee fellow was listening to the yarn — Says he, "I'll take it to you if you get me a horse and a couple of coppers."

'"I'll get the horse for you," says the merchant.

'He got the old horse and the saddle and put the wee fellow up on it and he dodged off, heading for Newry to get his money. And when he went down to the finger-post below, who did he meet only this gentleman coming walking along the road and he stopped him, stopped the lad, do you know, and asked him where he was going. "I'm going to Newry," he says, "for money for a merchant in Dundalk and I'm afraid of my life," says he, "to meet this Redmond O'Hanlon."

'"Oh," he says, "I'll be here and Redmond'll not touch you."

'And who was he talking to only Redmond!

'He went on ahead to Newry and got his money from the merchant anyhow and he hung the bag of coppers on the point of the saddle and put the other money in under the saddle and when he came up there to the half-way house, just coming round the corner, who did he meet only Redmond on horseback. "Your money now," he says, "or your life!"

'"Well," says the wee fellow, "I never handed money into a man's hand in my life, nor I'm not going to do it now." And he stood up and he fired the bag of coppers away into the wood. Redmond jumped off his horse to go in for the gold and he got down off his old horse and got up on Redmond's one and hit Dundalk and Redmond couldn't catch him.'[5]

It's a long way from Kilworth, just north of the town of Fermoy in County Cork, to Crieff in the Scottish Highlands but distance is no object to good stories and good songs and it is hardly surprising to read that in

Crieff at Hogmanay in the days when 'bevies of young men and maidens dressed themselves in the most ridiculous apparel their imaginations could suggest and securing, where possible, the services of a fiddler went about visiting the different houses in the country, dancing and singing songs;' one of the most popular songs they sang was what they called *Bold Brannin on the Moor*. In Ireland, the story and especially the song of 'Willie Brennan's wild career' remain popular to the present day.

D. J. Norris, writing in *The Shamrock* in 1875, summarised the career of this famous outlaw as follows:

'Willie Brennan was an outlaw of the Rob Roy school whose father was an affluent farmer by the banks of the famed Blackwater that flows to the sea, where it is said, Willie received a tolerable education in his youth. When troubles come we are told they come not in single files but in battalions and they came upon the Brennan household so rapidly that his father was soon ranked among the reduced farmers.

'One fine morning while still a young man, Willie Brennan was witness to an Irish eviction. His father was dispossessed. His mother was taken from her sick couch and saved from homelessness and want by the generous love and hospitality of the people. But her death followed quickly upon the event and thenceforward Willie Brennan was an outlaw, resolved to protect the poor from the despotism of petty tyrants. He took to his native hills and in a short space of time had surrounded himself with a trusty gang of men injured as he had been and desperate as he was himself. No oath it is said bound them together but they were simply in league to defend the helpless peasantry against the persecutions of the vampire aristocracy in Ireland. Few names evoked more popularity than that of the rapparee Captain, Willie Brennan.

13

'Unlike the celebrated Freeney or O'Hanlon, Brennan was no mere freebooter. He was a man of lofty purpose and took the law into his own hands only when it refused to afford him protection. Loyal to the cause of the country and faithful to the poor and the oppressed, he could always place implicit confidence in the people who guarded him from the vigilant enemies that were always on his path and the people always had a welcome for him in their hearts and in their homes.

'His birthplace was Kilworth, some two miles north of Fermoy, County Cork, and this was also the haunt of this famous highwayman. His exploits were all of a chivalrous character and he had a great aversion to the shedding of blood. His popularity with the peasantry was immense. One day he was met by two officers of the Fermoy garrison who recognised him by means of previous description, accused him of highway robbery and arrested him in the Queen's name. Willie was caught off guard and offered no resistance, merely saying — "Is it a poor boy like me to be the bold Brennan?"

'On their way to the garrison they soon reached a shebeen where Willie requested permission to light his pipe. All three entered the cabin in which for many a year he had been no stranger, when Willie, handing his pipe to the barmaid and looking at her with peculiar significance said, "Put fire in that." She understood the hint and presently returned with his blunderbuss concealed beneath her apron which she managed to hand him under the table. "Now, gentlemen," he exclaimed, covering his guards with the formidable weapon, as he rose, "I am the bold Brennan." The tables were completely turned, the captors became captive, yielded their money and their arms and were suffered to return to their quarters quite crestfallen.

'Perhaps the most singular feature of Brennan's wild career was his reluctance to shedding blood. His entire band shared in the chivalry and benevolence of his character but there was one of them who went by the name of the Pedlar Bán to whom Brennan was particularly attached. The manner of their first meeting was as follows. It chanced that Pedlar Bán found himself belated in a lonely part of the Glen of Araglyn when he was accosted by none other than Willie Brennan himself. Ignorant of the outlaw's identity the Pedlar became delighted with his companion and they travelled on till the sun rose upon the cloud-capped summit of Galtee More. They had not been long together when Brennan in sportive mood deprived the Pedlar of his valuable watch and chain. The latter remained unconscious of his loss but when he did discover it, he kept the discovery to himself and waited a favourable opportunity of which he made use in his turn to rob the rapparee of both watch and chain again. The subtle ingenuity of the Pedlar captured Brennan's admiration. He induced him to join his gang and sharing together in every daring deed, they remained firm friends until the capture of Captain Willie Brennan led to the disbanding of the outlaws.

'Large rewards were frequently offered by the government for his capture and there was no better proof of his popularity or the high esteeem in which he was held by the people than the fact that for nigh a score years they had been offered in vain. At length, however, he was betrayed. One night, in the depth of winter, he took refuge in a cottage at the foot of Galtee More, whose occupant was a woman of unsettled habits, no less, in fact, than a relative of the famous Moll Dunbar. who swore away the life of the noble patriot priest, Father Sheehy, in Clonmel. She had been the frequent recipient of Brennan's bounty, and, doubtless, she would be one of the last persons he would suspect of treachery to himself. On the evening in question, he slept very soundly, seeing which his crafty and ungracious hostess conceived the notion of betraying her benefactor and of earning the blood money offered for his capture. First she wet the powder in the pan of his blunderbuss and then she crept stealthily forth to acquaint the soldiery that the dauntless outlaw was at their mercy. The troopers came and laid hands upon him while he slept, but nevertheless, Brennan made a gallant struggle for his liberty. Laying hold of his trusty weapon and finding that it hung fire, he seized some rude instrument of defence with which he brought down several of his opponents and afterwards, it was often said that the first blood shed by Willie Brennan was the blood he shed in his last defence. There was no possibility of overpowering the number of his assailants so that he was finally captured and in a brief time, after a routine trial had been gone through, the eventful life of the rapparee Captain, Willie Brennan was terminated upon the public scaffold in Clonmel.'[6]

Further west in County Cork lived Seán Rua, alias John Murphy, of Macroom, who like Willie Brennan owed his life to a quick-witted servant girl. She it was who warned him by her clever use of Irish of the danger he was in when he once sought shelter and sustenance in a certain house in the locality. The words she spoke were remembered in the chorus of a song once famous in that part of the world. *'Más maith leat a bheith buan,'* said she, *'caith fuar agus teich!* The servant girl's words were deliberately ambiguous, for they could be taken to mean, 'If you wish to live long, drink cold and hot (*te*)' or as she wanted Seán Rua to understand, 'If you want to live long, drink cold and run (*teich*).' Fortunately, Seán Rua took the hint and made good his escape.

The same Seán Rua when in want of food, used to send his dog into Macroom with a basket tied round his neck. The basket would be filled by sympathetic shopkeepers and the dog would then trot back to its master's hiding place. When followed by people anxious to capture Seán Rua, the dog was known to have led his trackers into swamps and quagmires eventually giving them the slip and thus saving his master's bacon.[7]

Quick thinking was a very necessary attribute for any outlaw anxious to keep one step ahead of his pursuers. Michael Collier, who died in 1849, and who was called 'the last of the Irish highwaymen' — and also, simply, 'Collier the Robber' by his contemporaries — was no exception in this regard. He 'worked' the roads of Cavan, Louth, Meath and north County Dublin where, it was said, he had many friends among the ordinary people. Once while being hotly pursued by the forces of law and order, he arrived in a field where a number of men and women were digging potatoes. He boldly announced who he was and threw himself at the mercy of the people. In a moment, and just as the pack of soldiers appeared, he was placed in a pit and covered with potatoes, only one small hole being left in his impromptu covering.[8]

Collier, who turned informer and police spy, ended his days in relative comfort, whereas Charles O'Dempsey, otherwise known as *Cathaoir na gCapall*, on account of his weakness for horse-stealing, was hanged in Maryborough in 1734. Cathaoir had a way with horses and was able to tame the wildest colts ever foaled by means of a charm which he had. No matter how wicked or obstinate his mount might be, before they parted company, he was always master. On more than one occasion he is said to have fooled his pursuers by switching his horse's shoes back to front to lay a false trail and once while imprisoned awaiting trial for the theft of a certain bit of horseflesh with very peculiar markings, he contrived to have a mare, more or less similarly marked, substituted for the horse in question. The evidence against him broke down when the 'horse' the owner subsequently swore to be his own property turned out on inspection to be a mare![9]

Nevertheless, for all their flamboyance, the deeds of neither Michael Collier nor *Cathaoir na gCapall* are remembered in song, to the best of my knowledge, but those of Ned of the Hill, or *Éamonn an Chnoic,* are. Of all the Irish rapparees, he cuts the most romantic figure, a feature emphasised in this account of his career taken down in his own native Tipperary and preserved in the folklore manuscripts at University College, Dublin:

'Ned was born in Templebeg, County Tipperary over on the Borrisokane side. He was one of the Ryans of the Hill — every Ryan had a nickname. It would seem that these Ryans were in affluent circumstances and young Éamonn was intended for the priesthood. He got whatever book learning he could at home and was then sent off to France to be finished off and to be ordained. I needn't tell you there were no big colleges in Ireland at that time and £5 was the price for the head of a priest and for the head of a wolf.

'Young Ned's father fell sick and he was called home from France to receive his father's blessing. It happened while he was at home that the sheriff came to seize the only cow of a widow in the district. The neighbours gathered up and drove away the bailiffs and one of the bailiffs was killed and Éamonn was blamed for it. He had to take to the hills and that was goodbye to the priesthood for him. He joined the rapparees, Galloping Hogan and the others, and spent most of his life an outlaw chasing the English and helping the poor. Some will tell you that he was in Limerick with Sarsfield and that he was as far afield as the Boyne. There is no doubt that he helped to guide Sarsfield to Ballyneety, anyway. It would seem that he managed to work his land by times for many a year to come and he became engaged to a neighbouring girl, one Eibhlín Ryan. Éamonn got poorer and poorer as you might expect and my bold Eibhlín hadn't half the *grá* for him then as she had before. She began to set her cap for an English officer and finally ran off with him, I believe, though she didn't have a day's luck for giving the back of her hand to Ned of the Hill.

'Ned's relatives coveted his bit of land and in the heel of the hunt they wouldn't have been above selling him for the blood money. There was a price on his head you know — £30 — but that was a lot of money in those days.

'When Ned was hard pressed by government agents and by his own relatives he had to go for a while back to the Borrisokane district where he put up with a kinswoman of his own. Her husband was not told who the visitor was and Ned used to spend a lot of his time out about the hills and only came back for his food and to have a good sleep at night. These poor people never had such a time before with venison and all kinds of game and salmon from the river, for Ned had a gentleman's taste for the goods things of this world, moreover he was a crack shot and an expert fisherman.

'At last the man of the house got suspicious and went in and lodged information in the barracks at Cashel. Next morning, a company of soldiers arrived, but Ned just had time to slip out the back window and hide in a barrel until he got an opportunity to make good his escape altogether.

'Some years later, the man of the house in which Ned had taken refuge died and was buried in Upperchurch. Next morning, his body was found outside the wall of the graveyard. It was re-interred but the same thing happened again the next night and eventually all they could do was to make a grave outside the wall and leave the betrayer of Ned of the Hill there to await the final trumpet. I wouldn't say that Ned had hand act or part in removing the body from consecrated ground.

'Ned used to put up here and there — a different place every night. He used to leave his horse tied to the door outside and sleep on the kitchen table fully dressed with his weapons all ready beside him. This night he put up with a full cousin of his own and he wasn't long asleep when he awoke with a start. Ned's horse was neighing outside and he was on the point of going out but his cousin assured him that there was no danger and that he would keep watch till morning. Ned fell asleep again but the horse started neighing worse than ever. "I was dreaming," said Ned, "that there was a man going to cut the head off me."

'"Nonsense, man," said the cousin, "you are perfectly safe."

'Ned fell asleep again but the horse would give him no rest and he jumped up from the table and faced his cousin. Before Ned could draw his sword or pick up a gun, his own cousin swiped the head off him with an axe.

'The cousin buried Ned's body in Curraheen, where you can see Ned of the Hill's grave to the present day, and started for Clonmel with the head in a bag. When he got to Clonmel all he could do was to throw the head into the river and come back. Ned had been pardoned the day before. Ned's sister, walked the whole cut to Clonmel and brought home her brother's head and the body was dug up and buried along with the head in Toem and for some reason or other it was lifted again after that and buried in the old graveyard in Doon.'

This traditional account of Ned's career and downfall goes on to tell us how Ned came to be pardoned in the first place.

'Two English officers, it seems, were out shooting game on the mountains. They were firing all morning but they couldn't get near enough to the game and they had two empty bags. They met up with this tall young *cábóg* dressed in an old ragged *cóta mór*. "Come with me, gentlemen," said he, "and I'll show you where you'll get plenty of game." They were afraid to go with him at first for they thought he might be leading them into a trap but eventually they agreed to follow the ill-dressed youth and see what would happen. He brought them to where the game was as thick as stars in a March sky and they began firing and reloading and firing again and it wasn't long until they had plenty of game but they still were missing some of the best birds. "Give me a gun," said the youth, "and I'll teach you how to drop them." One of the officers handed Ned his gun and they never saw such shooting before. "One would almost think you were Ned of the Hill you have such a great shot," said the officer in open admiration. Ned smiled but said nothing.

'By and by, when the two guns were empty, Ned jumped up on a nearby bank and throwing aside his old coat stood there six foot of as fine a boy as they ever clapped eyes on with two pistols ready and primed stuck in his belt. "Now, gentlemen," said he drawing the pistols from his belt, "take your first and last look at Ned of the Hill." The two officers were dumbfounded but they stood up like men to face their doom.

'Ned stuck the pistols back in his belt and said: "I have no intention of shooting you now. I could have done that all morning while I was watching you."

'The upshot of the matter was the Ned and the officers sat down to picnic together out on the mountain and before they took farewell of one another, Ned told them how to get out of the mountains in safety and wrote them a pass saying that no man was to molest a hair of their heads. From that day forward those two officers left no stone unturned in their efforts to get a free pardon for Ned of the Hill, a pardon, which eventually came too late.'[10]

Hags and Hares

Wise women and hags, women supposed to have the evil eye or second sight, and women stealers of milk or butter 'profit' are but some of the categories of females whose persons are surrounded by mystery and accounts of whose supranormal activities form such an important part of the Irish folk tradition. As any folklore collector worth his salt will tell you, individuals of this ilk are still widely talked about in many parts of the country. It may not even be too much of an exaggeration to say that these women and their doings not only constitute a continuing subject of conversation in a good many parts of this island, but that actually a lot of people still go in fear and dread of warranting their attention.

Nearly forty years ago, the Folklore of Ireland Society published Seán Ó Súilleabháin's monumental treatise on Irish folklore — *A Handbook of Irish Folklore*.[1] This remarkable book contains what amounts to a step by step guide to the huge manuscript holdings of the former Irish Folklore Commission over which Seán presided for many years as archivist. The *Handbook* is not only a guide but it is also a compendium of all the myriad aspects of folk tradition in Ireland. In it, Seán Ó Súilleabháin lists a variety of misfortunes which, it was widely believed, could be brought about by female sorcerers.[2] Such individuals could achieve the death of an enemy by boiling water from a well in the name of the devil or by destroying a picture or image of the person in question or by holding a mock wake over a sheaf of straw which was intended to represent him. Women like this could raise a wind by tying and untying certain knots on a rope or handkerchief or by turning certain stones or by burying a cat alive in sand *and*, if

22

they felt like it, they could do such tricks as arranging to
see the wind by sucking the teats of a sow after she had
given birth to a litter of bonhams. As was the case with
their male counterparts, female sorcerers could acquire
all sorts of extraordinary power and knowledge by
selling themselves to the devil. Boiling pins or washing
clothes, especially shifts, in his name, was one specifi-
cally female way of making an approach to Old Nick.
All manner of ill luck and misfortune could be called
down upon neighbours by burying certain objects on
their land or even simply by rubbing feet on a
neighbour's threshold. Ships could be sunk and drown-
ing caused by sailing a small vessel in a container of boiling water until it eventually sank beneath the surface.
Conception and childbirth could be prevented by tying a
knot on a string during the marriage ceremony or by
secretly tying a withy round one of the rafters in the
house in which the couple who were the object of
malicious intentions of this kind lived.

To crown it all, it was said that the perpetrators of all
such evil actions also had the power to render themselves invisible by the use of fern seed. The hardy individual who elected to undertake this dangerous task was
supposed to repair alone, shortly before midnight on
Hallowe'en, to the solitary place where the ferns were
growing, armed with a number of pewter plates, all
regularly laid or imposed over one another and with a
sheet of white linen or paper placed between the two
lower ones. These plates were held under the fern and,
precisely at the hour of midnight, the seed was dropped
and so great was its enchanted power that it was able to
pass through all the plates except the lowermost one
where it was caught on the linen or paper. All the
powers of darkness and evil, it was said, would be mus-
tered to frighten off anyone brave enough to venture out
in pursuit of this magic fern seed and as the hour of

midnight approached, the air would be filled with yells and screams, whirlwinds, thunder and lightning and ghostly apparitions.[3]

Wise women, hags and witches — often referred to in the province of Connacht in an act of linguistic hand-washing as *Na Mná Muimhneacha* (The Munster Women) and *Cailleacha Chúige Uladh* (The Ulster Hags) — are not the only females to be viewed with suspicion in Irish tradition, for even ordinary women sometimes were tarred with this same brush. It was considered a bad omen, for example, for a woman to be the first to enter a house on New Year's Day and women, especially red-haired women, brought nothing only bad luck to fishermen about to put to sea and to people on their way to fairs and markets who were unfortunate enough to meet up with them along the way. A whistling woman or a woman who happened to be the first person one met when taking a child to be baptised was to be avoided every bit as energetically as one would seek to avoid the imposition of the famous 'widow's curse'. Not even the celebrated notion of the 'woman's touch' escapes unscathed, for it is recorded that rat-banishing clay or sand such as that found on Inisglora, off the Mayo coast, or on Tory Island, off the north coast of Donegal, immediately loses its efficacy if stepped upon by a woman.

This is a sorry catalogue, indeed, misogynistic even, though it is only fair to say that traditional beliefs and attitudes such as these are not only ascribable to the Irish, but that they are really international in character. Many of the charges here levelled against womenkind and the evil qualities imputed to members of the fair sex are also frequently credited against members of the male sex. Nevertheless, it must be said that the overall impression is of a negative, even malign role for women within the tradition.

Traditionally, as we all know, a woman's place was in the home and one of her most important duties there was the business of making butter. Consistent success at churning was a crucial economic factor in country life in days gone by and it is no wonder that this was an enterprise hedged around by prohibitions and surrounded by rituals every bit as bizarre as a Common Market butter mountain. 'Taking a brash' at the churn, that is to say volunteering to take a hand at the actual churning process, was a gesture expected from any visitor to a house where churning was in progress and, of course, the traditional *Bail ó Dhia ar an obair* (God bless the work) was a greeting not to be omitted on any account on such occasions. The taking of preventive action to neutralise possible outside interference in the work, interference which might lead to endless churning but a complete absence of butter, was also a common practice. It usually took the form of a tongs or live coal from the fire being placed under the churn while it was being operated, but in some cases only the traditional power of the iron and the glowing coal in tandem were sufficient to stand in the way of malicious neighbours hell bent on stealing your butter.

Pádraig Eoghan Phádraig Mac an Luain, from the melodiously named townland of Crooveenananta in the heart of the Blue Stack Mountains in Donegal, often talked about this subject and I was fortunate enough to be able to record some of that lore from him. Though he was in his nineties at the time, he was a man still possessed with great vigour and a wry sense of humour, not to mention a dazzling command of his native dialect of Irish which was, in fact, the only language he knew. Here (translated from the Irish) is a story on this theme which I recorded from him in 1972:

'Well, these women were just ordinary country women like you still see around except that they were able to work this magic, whatever way they did it. If you had cows, they could take the "profit" of them from you. The milk you got from the cows would be useless, insipid and lifeless, and they would have the butter for themselves.

'There was a man living near here one time and he had eight cows. Day in day out, he used to see this hare running about, in and out among the cows in his fields. He didn't know what the hare was doing there, but he did notice that he was making nothing from the milk his cows were giving — it was just like water.

'He had a dog, a pure black hound, and they say that a hound without a speck of white in it that has a rod of the rowan tree tied around its neck is the only animal that can catch a hare like that. So one day when he saw the hare among the cows, he loosed the hound after her. Hound and hare coursed the fields back and forward and finally the hare made to jump over a high stone wall and the hound caught her by the leg and broke it. The man knew that the hound had caught the hare and when he came up to where they were what did he find there only an old hag who lived in the locality sitting by the wall with the blood pouring out of her.

'The hag was brought home and some time after that she died and the man went to the wake. They were going round with the whiskey at the hag's wake and he was offered a glass too. "Here, drink a glass for the old woman," they said.

'"Indeed, I won't," said he, "for I got my fill of her."'

On that same occasion, Pádraig followed this up by reciting another anecdote dealing with the same subject. Here it is translated from the Irish:

'May morning was a terrible time for working charms of all kinds but especially for stealing the "profit" of your milk. One May morning this man was coming up

through Altnapaste and he saw this hag, back and forward through a field, pulling an iron chain after her and
this is what she was saying: "Come all to me, come all to
me." The man was riding on horseback on the road and
watching all this and he shouts: "The half of it for me."

'That was all there was to that but when he got home
he noticed that his cows had an awful lot of milk. All the
vessels he had about the house were filled to overflow-
ing with milk. He told the priest about it and eventually
things were put right again. He had got half of what the
old hag had been asking for herself.'

On another occasion, Pádraig told me the story of
what he called *An Maistreadh Mór* (The Big Churning)
in which he described how a family which had suffered
the attention of a butter-stealing hag, and had been
nearly beggared as a result, was finally forced to take the
awful step of working *An Maistreadh Mór* — a powerful
charm — against the unknown predator in an effort to
put a stop to her activities. One day before they com-
menced their regular churning, they began to redden a
donkey's shoe in the fire and while it was growing hot
they saw to it that all the doors and windows in the house
were tightly secured so that no one could get in. Then
they placed the red hot donkey's shoe under the churn
and began their usual churning. No time after that, a
woman was heard screeching and hammering at the
door, begging to be let in. The poor woman was in
agony from the effects of the red hot shoe on her body
for that was what she had experienced while engaged in
her customary butter-stealing exercise. Who was it only
the next door neighbour! 'I knew her daughter well,'
declared Pádraig with a chuckle.

Monies that accrued from the sale of farm produce,
such as eggs and butter, were generally regarded as
belonging to the woman of the house, who was entitled
to dispose of them as she saw fit. Selling the produce

sometimes brought difficulties to people with an in-adequate knowledge of English — the language of commerce even in the vicinity of strong Irish-speaking areas — as this story (translated from the Irish) taken down by former Irish Folklore Commission collector, Liam Mac Coistealbha, in Claregalway, County Galway, reveals.

'There was once a farmer's wife on the Tuam road, a well-off woman with five or six head of milch cows. She was well-to-do and there wasn't a Saturday in the year that she wouldn't have plenty of butter to sell in Galway and every Saturday without fail she used to go there with her butter.

'She had a servant girl and it was only once in a wonder that the servant girl would be sent to the market for she knew no English. But, this Friday, the woman of the house said that she wasn't feeling too well and that she wouldn't be able to go to the market in Galway the following Saturday and she ordered the girl to do the selling instead and told her to be ready early in the morning.

'"What business would I have there," said the servant girl, "for if I met someone that only spoke English I wouldn't know what he was saying and I wouldn't be able to sell to him!"

'"All you have do do," says the woman of the house — butter was cheap in those days — "is to ask him for 'sixpence ha' penny', and, of course if he doesn't give it to you, some other person will — 'somebody else will'."

'"Is that all I have to say?" said the girl. "That's it," said the woman of the house.

'You never saw a happier girl than that girl going to Galway. She got ready early in the morning and put the butter in her basket and slung her basket over her back, and as she was heading down Bohermore, what did she meet but a young gentleman on a hunter heading for the country to hunt. He wasn't sure whether he should take the road east or whether he should head by Castlegar and he drew up as she was passing by.

'"Is this the road to Tuam?" says he.

'"Butter, sir!" says she.

'"What butter are you saying?" says he.

'"Sixpence ha'penny," says she.

'"Is it humbugging me you are?" says he. "Only I'm loath I'd come down and whip you with the whip!"

'"If you don't," says she, "another will."

'He jumped down off his horse and hit her four or five cracks of his whip and he laid her out. The butter prints fell out of her basket and the Bohermore terriers started into the butter when they got the smell of it and they didn't leave a bit of it that they didn't eat. That's how she got on. She had to head back without either butter or money.'[4]

Further south in County Kerry, P. J. O'Sullivan of Annascaul reports on a shady individual who was intent on making a fast buck in the butter market but who turned out in the end to be just as unsuccessful in this line of business as the innocent and unfortunate servant girl in Galway.

'There was a boy out rambling one night and as he was coming home along the road, he heard someone talking inside the ditch. The boy stopped and listened a while and then he looked inside the ditch and he saw two hares inside. He was very surprised to hear two hares talking but he stood there listening to what they were saying, nevertheless. One hare said to the other: "We'll have a big meeting in such and such a place tonight for the enchanted wizard Murrough is coming to give us a lecture about milking cows and taking away butter from people." The boy stood there where he was and waited to see what would turn up. He wasn't long waiting till he saw that there were crowds and crowds of hares coming into the field and it wasn't long till the place was full of hares.

'One of the hares said that it wouldn't be long until the wizard Murrough came and indeed shortly after that a stranger came along the road on horseback with a big long whip in his hand. When he came to the field where the hares were he jumped over the ditch and he said to the hares that they could not hold their meeting in that field because it was too near the road. They were to come with him to another field farther away, "And," said Murrough, "if there are any of you here that aren't enchanted, say these three magic words after me and you will become enchanted." He said the magic words and the boy said them too and he was made into a hare also. As soon as he became a hare, he jumped into the field among all the other hares and not one of them took any notice of him.

'"Now," says Murrough, "all of you are enchanted, so come along with me to such and such a field and on your way you can milk all the cows that you meet." All the hares started off and the boy was the loosest of them all and they milked all the cows that they met in the fields along the way until at last they came to a certain field and they all sat down to listen to the wizard Murrough. "I am very sorry," said Murrough, "but I can't give you any lecture tonight because I know that there is some-one listening and I can't say a thing to you tonight. But, be here again tomorrow night at the same time and we'll see what we can do."

'All the hares went off home and the boy went home too and when he came to near his own place he said the magic words and he came back to his own shape again. He went in home and he said nothing about where he'd been or what he'd seen.

'The next night he headed off out the road again and he said the magic words and he turned himself into the

30

shape of a hare and he made his way along to the appointed meeting place of the night before. When he came into the field he saw a huge crowd of hares there but none of them took any notice of him and after a while, Murrough, the wizard, arrived riding as usual on a fine black horse. He got down off the horse and stood on a big rock that was there in the field. "Now," says he, "I am very sorry that I can't say anything to you tonight either because I know by the power of my magic that there's someone listening to us tonight and I can't say anything to you about the subject I was going to talk to you about. But if you come again tomorrow night I'll tell you all I know, so be sure and be here again at the same hour."

'All the hares promised him to come again and they all went off home and the boy went home too. He said the magic words and he changed into himself again. He didn't say a word to anyone about where he had been because he wanted to keep it a dead secret for he was sure that he would have great power if he went to the field the following night and, by the magic he would learn, he would be able to do lots of things that no one else could do and he would be rich beyond belief for ever more.

'When the next night came, the boy was in great hopes. He headed off out the road and said the magic words and he turned himself into the shape of a hare once again. He ran away across the fields until he reached the assembly field of the night before, and there he saw the same crowd of hares gathered and waiting. They weren't long waiting when Murrough appeared on his black horse. He got down off the horse and went up on top of the same big rock. "Now," says he, "I have come here two nights before and I wasn't able to tell you any of my knowledge for I could feel that there was someone listening to us. I have sent you home two nights before and now you have come the third night and I promise you that I will not let you go away this night empty-handed. First of all, let you all sit down in the field in rows and I'll tell you then what I'm going to do."

'All the hares sat down in rows and Murrough got up on his horse and took his whip in his hand and said: "By the power of my magic, I have found out that there is someone listening to us also tonight. But I will soon find out who it is and when I do, this person will pay sorely for it." He took out a small black book from his pocket and he started reading some magic words that no one could understand and when he had finished reading he put the book back into his pocket again and he said: "Now, by the power of my book of magic I have found out that it is not any man, woman or child that is listening to us but it is some stranger who by some magic powers or other has managed to turn himself into a hare and he has been amongst us every night we have been here and that was the reason I couldn't say anything. Do not fret, however, for I'll find out that hare very soon, so let all of you stay where you are and let me do the rest."

'Murrough began riding up and down on his black horse between the lines of hares drawn up in the field looking on every side for a sign of the strange hare. At last he came up to where the boy was in the shape of a hare and by his magic power he knew that this was the strange hare he was looking for. "Oh," says Murrough, "here he is. I have found him at last and now I'll make him pay for this work."

'He took out his whip and he drew at the hare with one blow and the hare jumped up and ran away. But Murrough followed him across the fields and as fast as the hare could run, Murrough was able to keep up with him and he kept lashing him with his whip all the while till the hare was sore and well bruised. When he had hunted him a great distance away, he stopped and he told the hare that he had got enough now and not to have the devil pick him to come back again for if he did he wouldn't get off as lightly as he did this time. The boy was very glad to be let off so lightly and he ran off home and saying the magic words immediately returned to his own shape and form.

'But I'm telling you that his ribs were sore for a few days after because of the whipping he got and as long as he lived he never attempted to turn himself into a hare again after the fright he got from Murrough.'[5]

The Day of the Horse

In the day of the horse, blacksmiths, harness-makers and saddlers were to be found in every town in Ireland. When horses supplied the power on the farm, the premises of these craftsmen fairly hummed with business, as they fixed shoes and repaired all the main gears required by farm horses — collars, hames, saddles and breechings, traces and reins. Nowadays, only a scattering of farmers follow the plough and what farm horses remain have mostly been put out to graze and left just as idle as the surviving few harness-makers who used to follow what was once a thriving trade.

The vision of man and horse teamed up together to work the land for profit has been replaced by the modern-day reality of man riding in the countryside for pleasure. Nevertheless, whether it be from behind the plough or at riding school or racetrack, now as always, the horse exudes a remarkable mystique and exercises an extraordinary attraction for human kind. From the folklore point of view, there is any amount of popular tradition attaching to this animal — horses were generally believed to be susceptible and sensitive to the power and , sence of all manner of otherworld beings; they could be stopped short in their tracks, for example, by mysterious forces and obstacles, invisible to the human eye, and they were frequently singled out as victims of fairy malice of one kind or another and of the evil eye. Then there is the phenomenon of 'true mares' as they were called — the seventh consecutive filly born to a dam; these were thought of as being a kind of superhorse, invincible against all kinds of hostile spirits and prodigious racers to boot. There are also many accounts detailing the skills of whisperers — men who could calm the wildest and most nervous of young horses by whispering in their ears. The horse's acute sense of smell is also a feature frequently commented upon as too are cures for all kinds of equine ailments from strained muscles to saddle gall and sore breast. It is, indeed, a rich and varied catalogue of traditional skills, beliefs and crafts that surrounds this most appealing of all four-footed animals.[1]

Though most of the traditional crafts associated with the horse have fallen into decline and horses themselves become less and less visible on the streets of our cities and towns, the business of buying and selling horse-flesh still goes on unabated. It is a business, let it be said, that is fraught with danger and full of pitfalls for the unwary and the untutored in the art of judging the true qualities of any animal in the market place.

According to tradition, when selling a horse one should never give the halter away. To break this basic ground rule would bring endless bad luck, it was believed. It was, of course, also often said that one should never give anything before selling or, to put it another way, 'you should always get before you give'.

At fair or market, people did not like to part with goods or money until they had first sold some of their own stock or produce. Women, in particular, often made an elaborate pretence of having to borrow a safety-pin to fasten their shawls, in this manner managing to satisfy the traditional requirement that they should get before they gave.

Talking of halters, it is also worth noting the widespread belief that a horse should never be struck with its own halter, a belief often advanced in stories like the one from Killasser, County Mayo, which tells us what happened to a man who lived there long ago and who once struck his favourite mare with her halter as he was letting her and her foal out to graze. Mare and foal immediately made for a nearby lake, and in the twinkling of an eye, disappeared into it. Every night, they used to return to graze on dry land, but no one ever succeeded in catching them again until one night, the Killasser man managed to break the spell by once again striking the mare with her own halter thus causing mare and foal to abandon their watery abode and return to their ordinary life on dry land.[2] This story incorporates elements of the common belief that lakes and rivers all over the country were infested with water horses who came out to graze at night, sometimes mating with the local breed of mares to produce extraordinary offspring. It was said, too, that if you were foolish enough to approach these water horses during their nocturnal grazing, that with the intake of one gigantic breath, they could draw you into the water after them.

The business of buying and selling has spawned many stories, especially stories describing the dubious activities of smart Alecs, fly-by-nights and other 'Trick of the Loop' men. Here is one about a fellow called 'Innocent Johnny' who was sent to sell a horse at the fair of Skryne in County Meath. He sold the animal without much trouble and having done so was asked by the incautious buyer — on whom a small suspicion that he had just been tricked, in some way or other, was slowly dawning — if the horse had any faults.

'I don't know,' said Innocent Johnny.

'You do know,' said the buyer, 'and I'll give you ten bob for yourself if you tell me.'

'Fair enough,' said Johnny, 'hand over the money and I'll tell you.'

The buyer gave Johnny the ten shillings for himself. 'Tell me his faults, now,' said he.

'Well, now,' said Innocent Johnny, 'it's like this — this horse is a bit forgetful.'

'What do you mean?' said the buyer.

'Well,' said Johnny, 'if you give him a crack of the whip, he'll forget it in a few minutes and, what's more, he's very hard to catch, but when he's caught, you'll hardly see him stir when you have him yoked!'

Innocent Johnny wasn't so innocent at all, in the heel of the hunt.[3]

He had a counterpart in County Longford, it seems, a man who was unfortunate enough to own a horse which, as they say, would kick the stars off the sky and couldn't be made to work in any shape or form. This 'Longford' Johnny decided to bring his horse to the fair in the hope of getting rid of him and, sure enough, he found a buyer who wanted an engagement. The engagement he got guaranteed that the horse in question would do as much work for the smallest child in the house as for himself, and the deal was made and the horse bought on that basis. It was challenged afterwards in court, but, according to the judge, the terms of 'Longford' Johnny's engagement held good.[4] Court is where another Irish farmer who had a cow which was almost impossible to milk might have landed too, if there is any truth in the following story. His cow was so restless that no one could succeed in milking her and at last he said he would sell her. He sent his servant boy to the fair with her and some time later he returned home with a lot more money that the farmer had expected to get for her. 'Did you tell the truth about the cow?' said the farmer. 'I did,' replied the servant-boy. 'The man asked me if she gave plenty of milk and I said, "Man, you'll be tired to death with the milking of her!"'[5]

Some years ago, I recorded another couple of 'horsey' stories from the late Pádraig Eoghan Phádraig Mac an Luain of Donegal. Echoes of a time when cattle raids across the Ulster/Connacht border were commonplace could sometimes be detected in Pádraig's stories, especially those in which *an Connachtach bradach* (the thieving Connachtman) — to use Pádraig's own term — played a leading role. One of these describes how an honest Ulsterman was almost deceived by a cute Connachtman from whom he had just agreed to buy a certain horse. The Ulsterman happened to overhear the Connachtman boasting to some of his compatriots that the horse which he had managed to get the Ulsterman to agree to buy was faulty. A little later, when it was time to pay for the animal in question, the Ulsterman proposed that they adhere to an ancient ritual which, he said, always accompanied horse-buying in the part of the world he came from. This ritual consisted of passing the money — the price of the horse — three times over and under the horse's body, repeating each time — *bíodh seo nó do chuid féin agat* (take this or keep your own). The Connachtman agreed to go along with this and as he handed the money over the horse's back into the hands of the Ulsterman for the third time and uttered the words of the formula — *bíodh seo nó do chuid féin agat* (take this or keep your own) — the Ulsterman speedily interjected — *beidh mo chuid féin agam* (I'll keep my own), seized back the purchase price and left the Connachtman standing there with his faulty horse and the deal called off — at his own invitation.

Pádraig's other 'horsey' story is of a somewhat more uplifting character, featuring not a thieving Connachtman but, on this occasion, a repentant one. This Ulsterman, it seems, went to a fair in Connacht to sell a fine black mare which he had and there he met up with a Connachtman who agreed to buy her on condition that he was allowed to ride her a bit first in order to try her out. The Ulsterman readily agreed and that was the last he saw of his mare, for the Connachtman never came back and he was forced to head back home without mare or money.

Some years after, a poor beggarman was going round the country, seeking lodgings here and there and it so happened that he used to spend a night, now and then, with the Ulsterman and also with the Connachtman. One time, the Connachtman asked him what was the most astonishing thing he had ever seen and the beggarman replied that it surely must be the sight of a certain Ulsterman, with whom he occasionally found shelter, going on his bended knees to say a special prayer every night for the spiritual and physical well-being of the Connachtman who had stolen his fine black mare.

Not long after that, the Ulsterman happened to be at a fair in Connacht again and who came up to buy a horse from him only this same Connachtman, though the Ulsterman didn't recognise him at the time. The Connachtman asked could he go for a ride on the horse to try him out, but the Ulsterman said he couldn't allow that for he had had a fine black mare stolen from him by giving in, once, to just such a request.

'Would you recognise that mare if you saw her again?' said the Connachtman.

'Indeed, I would,' said the Ulsterman.

There and then, the Connachtman produced the

black mare, complete with foal, from a nearby stable and handed them over to the Ulsterman. He took the mare, but not the foal, and that was the end of the whole affair.

These two stories and, indeed, a good many other stories, that Pádraig used to tell, probably date back to a time before the Famine, a time when the island of Ireland was peopled by eight million or more souls, a figure that was to be reduced by half in the space of a few generations. The darkest hours of those bad days were occasionally lightened by the good works of charitable bodies and individuals, people like Samuel Bournes, for example, Protestant landlord of Rossport, in the west of Ireland, and one-time owner of a famous racehorse, as this excellent account, written by Michael Corduff, also of Rossport, now reveals.

'During the years of the Great Famine around 1847, the late Samuel Bournes, landlord of Rossport in the Barony of Erris, in the County Mayo, was the dispenser of a large volume of relief to the local people. He obtained large quantities of food through the co-opera-tion of the Society of Friends, commonly known as Quakers, and this food he doled out chiefly to residents of his own estate, but he also supplied relief food to the destitute and hungry of outside areas. He kept a huge iron boiler constantly cooking Indian meal stirabout and many a hungry wayfarer had his hunger appeased thereat.

'Hence it was that Rossport in those days became the Mecca of the poor and the needy from various parts of the country and even whole families migrated to Rossport and settled down there. . .

'Samuel Bournes, landlord of Rossport, had a young mare which he himself broke in and trained. He was an excellent horseman and kept great horses. He was very proud of this young mare which was of a very fiery and high-spirited disposition. Her galloping speed was incredible and her capacity for clearing jumps, fences and gates was simply astonishing. Bournes raced her in Sligo, Ballina and Crossmolina as well as at other venues against some of the best blooded competitors of equine flesh in Mayo and adjoining counties and in those days the aristocracy bred some great horses, but the Rossport grey mare triumphed at all race meetings, hunts and jumping competitions.

'The owner, Mr Bournes, named the horse "Jenny Lind" after the great soprano singer of the day, who was popularly known as "The Swedish Nightingale" and it was around this time she achieved the summit of her fame. The horse was known by the people of Rossport as the "Jenna Lin" — very probably, they never knew who Jenny Lind was, or whence the name of the horse was derived, but the tenants on the estate had a strong attachment for the famous mare. In olden stories of the century and more old days of the famine times, the name of "Jenny Lind" the landlord's horse is preserved and perpetuated. The name "Jenny Lind" was a synonym for outstanding or conspicuous speed among horses. "The great 'Jenna Lin' would not keep with him" was a favourite expression in Irish to denote the speed of some quadruped, the comment being of course, mere hyperbole, and perhaps applied to a donkey and so it is that the speed of that famous horse has become legendary with the passage of time.

'Many extraordinary feats of jumping have been attributed to "Jenny Lind". She is reputed to have cleared the huge iron gate leading to Rossport House as well as many high stone walls and other almost insurmountable obstacles. These scenes of the steed's marvellous prowess are pointed out today for the edification of the younger people of the present generation and, certainly, if the fame of "Jenny Lind" is justified by fact as chroni-

cled in local tales, then there can be no doubt whatever
of the deserved fame of that great steed. But shrewd
judges shake their heads in misgiving, regarding the
alleged performances of the animal and give the opinion
that the deeds ascribed to that doubtless very worthy
animal have become grossly exaggerated in the century
that has elapsed in the interval.

'It is related that this extraordinary animal breathed
from its anus as well as from the mouth and that this is a
trait or physical characteristic not possessed by one
horse in a million. Any horse so distinctively endowed is
supposed to be possessed of well-nigh supernatural staying power, and if the stories of "Jenny Lind" be true,
then her speed and stamina are unparalleled in the
annals of equine records.

'On one occasion, she flew her rider, a young man
named Hogan of Rossport, who was a servant at the Big
House. He happened to be riding her along the road at
Rossport and, being a skilful and intrepid rider, he
galloped her towards the cross-roads of Rossport. She
was headed due north and towards the strand between
Rossport and Cornboy. When he thought to pull her up
or slacken speed, he found her uncontrollable. So she
ran away with him down the road, across the strand,
flew up the sandbanks of Garter Hill, descended into
the valley of Carratigue, crossed the terrain at the back
of that townland and came to rest when she floundered
in the soft bog of *Bogach an Tower*, overlooking the
high cliffs of the Atlantic. Were it not for the shaky and
impassable morass in which the horse sunk, it would
have continued its flight until it precipitated itself over
the thousand feet high cliff into destruction. The rider
afterwards said that he felt so hypnotised by the experi-
ence that he would have held onto the animal's back
until he would have gone over the cliff top into eternity.
But mercifully, rider and horse were saved from that

impending tragedy by the friendly quagmire in the vicinity of the ruined Martello tower.

'When rider and horse extricated themselves from the slimy marsh, Hogan turned the animal's head homewards and gave her plenty of rein, hoping to exhaust her, but instead of showing signs of weariness after her arduous and irksome race, she merely intensified her speed and, jumping across ditches and fields, hill and dale, shore and strand until again she stuck her hooves in Rossport soil, she actually flew with incredible speed. . . and only came to a standstill a short distance from the stable door. This was one of the horse's many noted escapades. . .

'It was believed that Mr Bournes cherished high hopes and ambitions for the career of "Jenny Lind" and that he intended entering her for the classic races in England and even had expectations of her winning at no distant date, the blue ribbon of the turf. . . but unfortunately that acme of the landlord's ambition was rather tragically denied to him. . . and the rosy anticipations entertained by him were. . . ruthlessly destroyed.

'It was about this time when hunger and famine and disease stalked the land which that good man, the landlord of Rossport, paradoxically as it seems, worked so assiduously and tirelessly to combat and ameliorate, that he one day received a letter by post from a high official of the Government or some philanthropic society — probably the Quaker Society — requesting Mr Bournes to meet him at Belmullet at an appointed hour on a certain date, to discuss means and measures to be adopted for the relief of the distressed and backward Erris area which was the primary concern of Mr Bournes in his benevolent activities.

'In those days, postal communication was slow, irregular and uncertain, particularly in backward areas of the country. . . The date and the hour for the conference between the representative and Mr Bournes was at twelve o'clock noon on the day the letter was delivered. It was then into the afternoon and Mr Bournes was much perturbed and disappointed in consequence. He had missed a great opportunity through the untimely arrival of the letter. However, he decided to proceed with all haste to Belmullet, in the hope of contacting the gentleman somewhere, either in the town or elsewhere. Accordingly he ordered that his favourite and fastest horse be got ready while he himself prepared for the journey with all possible haste, and so the fleet-footed "Jenny Lind". . . was hurriedly prepared for a fast journey to Belmullet. Mr Bournes, in order to save time, decided to swim the horse across Rossport Ferry and sent a special message to the ferrymen to have their boat in readiness when he and his horse arrived. . . It was her first essay in swimming across the ferry, but she accomplished the crossing without the slightest bother. . . [and] continued the journey to Belmullet with the maximum of speed in the minimum of time. It was defintely a race against time, or rather a race against lost time for, before he left his house, Mr Bournes was already hours late for the appointment and though he accomplished the journey in record time. he was, alas, too late. The gentleman whom he wished to meet had left for Killala some hours earlier. Undaunted by his disappointment, he decided to pursue his quarry to Killala hoping to catch up with him, either there or in Ballina. The journey to Killala, was, from Belmullet, over thirty [Irish] miles, but he had confidence in the ability and stamina of "Jenny Lind" in its achievement before nightfall.

'Again he took the road at a flying pace and careered wildly on his trusty steed, passing by houses and people along the north coast, at incredible speed, until he reached Killala, and to his jubilation, he then discovered that he had run his quarry to earth. He had overtaken the gentleman he was so extremely anxious to meet.

'At that time, a son of Mr Bournes — a Doctor William S. Bournes — was a resident practitioner in Killala and the landlord put up for the night at his son's house, and stabled his horse there. . . Later that evening, they [Mr Bournes and the visiting representative] met and conferred on the best ways and means of alleviating the distress in north-west Erris and talked the matter over long into the night. Owing to the absence of proper roads and the inaccessibilty of the area in question the problem of the transport of supplies created no small difficulty of solution. Food would have. . . to be carried by sea from the recognised depot at Westport and. . . so they planned out a scheme of transport by sea, which satisfactorily resolved what first seemed almost an insuperable obstacle to the success of the conference.

'Samuel Bournes was very well satisfied with the result of his day's work and at a late hour retired to the house of his son, the doctor, and went to bed. He was out of bed early next morning in accordance with his daily practice and his first concern was for the comfort and security of his horse, "Jenny Lind", which through her fleetness of foot the day before, had enabled him to bring the exertions of the day to such happy fruition.

'On entering the stable, to his dismay and horror, he found "Jenny Lind" stretched dead on the floor. Next to the death of a human being, no calamity could have distressed him more that the loss of this great horse, on which he had set such precious store. . . There was no blame or censure attaching to anyone in consequence but himself. He had over-driven her the previous day, on the long journey from Rossport to Belmullet, and thence to Killala and, as he himself observed in the course of condolences by his friends, she was sacrificed in a good cause. Her triumph in the achievement of the goal which had been set her the day before was the means of saving many lives during the ensuing year. Barring unforseen accidents there would be food for the people and no deaths from hunger during the trying months of the famine year which lay ahead.'

The ambitions which Samuel Bournes held for 'Jenny Lind', so cruelly frustrated, were to him a cause of poignant, though hidden sorrow, but in Black '47, no one died of starvation in Rossport or vicinity.[6]

Cats

It is curious how many expressions concerning cats occur in ordinary everyday speech. You have Cheshire cats and Kilkenny cats and, of course, the cat of nine tails. Depending on which way the cat jumps, you might say that care (or curiosity) killed the cat and satisfaction made him fight. There are cat's eyes, cat calls and cat's (or catch) cradle. 'Cat and dog' and 'Turning the Wildcat' are children's games, while a cat's paw is a name given to a patsy or a dupe after the fable about the monkey that used the paws of the cat to pull roasted chestnuts out of the fire. It has been known to rain cats and dogs and people occasionally let the cat out the bag. 'Would a cat drink sweet milk?' is a common way of confirming one's enthusiasm for some course of action or other while the dance tune title, *The Cat's Carrant through the Cream Crock*, further emphasises feline interest in that same commodity. Tom and Jerry cartoons are not normally referred to as the Cat and Mouse

Act, apt though that description might be for them, as for the following story taken down in 1936 by Tomás Ó Ciardha from Frank Cavanagh, then aged eighty-two, of Adamstown, County Wexford:

'Long ago, people used to make poteen around this district. There was a mouse, anyway, one time, and she fell into the wash and she couldn't get out. She was nearly drowned when who came along but the cat and he wasn't long pulling her out. The cat was going to kill her and eat her right away. "Musha," says the mouse, "it isn't worth your while killing me now. Wait for a few weeks till I get fat." The mouse was very wretched-looking after coming out of the wash.

'"All right," says the cat, "I'll let you go if you come out here in a month's time."

'"Very well," says the mouse.

'The cat let the mouse go anyway and she had a great time after that. She had plenty of milk and cheese and she was as fat as a roll of butter after a couple of weeks. When the month was up, the cat came along. The mouse came to the mouth of the hole but no farther. "Well," says the cat, "what way are you?"

'"Oh, I'm busting," says the mouse.

'"Well, are you coming out till I eat you," says the cat.

'"Indeed and I'm not," says the mouse, "what a quare thing I'd do!"

'"And didn't you promise this day month that if I let you go, you'd come out when you'd get fat?" said the cat.

'"Yerra, musha," said the mouse, "sure you wouldn't mind what I said that day, wasn't I as drunk as a stick!"'[1]

From County Cavan and the hand of P. J. Gaynor of Bailieborough, we have the following version of the famous story called 'Belling the Cat':

'There was a house one time and there was a lot of

mice about it. They were getting plenty to eat and they were having a fine time for there was no cat to annoy them. But, they were doing a lot of harm and the people of the house made up their minds to get a cat.

'The cat that they got turned out to be a great "mouser" and she was killing a good many of the mice. The mice were afraid of their lives and, eventually, they held a meeting to see what they could do about it. The head mouse made a speech and he talked about all of them that were getting killed and the danger it was for any of them to venture out and prowl around for something to eat. He asked if any of them could suggest some way of getting rid of the cat. None of them could think of any plan and they were all silent.

'At last, one mouse spoke up and says he: "I have a plan that will stop the cat from catching us."

'"What is it?" said the other mice.

'"Let's get a bell," said he, "and tie it round the cat's neck and when we find the bell jingling, we'll know that the cat's coming and we'll have time to get back into our holes."

'Nearly all the mice said it was a great plan and they were in great jubilation over it till one old mouse got up and asked: "Which of you is going to put the bell on the cat?" That put an end to that idea.

'There used to be a remark about that,' the storyteller went on, 'if you were after doing something that annoyed me or displeased me very much and I reprimanded you for it, it would be said that I "belled the cat" or if you were going to do something that shouldn't be done and I took courage and went to you and put you from doing it, it would be said that I "belled the cat".'[2]

'The Cat that Wanted the Pair of Shoes' is the title that Seán Ó Flanagáin gave to this story which he collected in 1937, from Séamas Ó Ceallaigh, aged forty-seven, a native of the Clare/Galway border country.

'This poor man lived out the mountain and he had three or four young children. Anyways, he kept an old cat and 'twas no knowing what big age the same cat had and the cat was able to talk like anyone.

''Twas in the winter time of the year and the father said he'd buy a pair of shoes each for the children in Gort. "Well, if you're going buying shoes for your children, you'll bring me a pair too," said the cat, "or if you don't I won't leave an eye in your children's heads!"

'"I won't be able to bring them to you today, but I'll have them for you next Saturday for sure," said the man of the house.

'"All right so," says the cat.

'The man of the house would not trust the cat and so he went out to a neighbour's house and told the neighbour to have an eye after the children while himself would be gone to Gort. Off he went to Gort and where Treston's shop is now, there was a bootmaker there long ago, and he went down to the bootmaker and bought four pairs of shoes for the children. "Well," says he to the bootmaker; "I have an old cat at home and she wants me to bring her a pair of boots and if I don't she won't leave an eye in the children's heads."

'"Well I'll tell you what you'll do," said the bootmaker. "Tell her that I can't make any boots for her until she comes in to me and gets her measure taken. Put her into a bag and be bringing her in to me and I'll have huntsmen and a pack of foxhounds ready to meet you on your way and if the captain asks you what is in the bag, tell him he can mind his own business or go to hell. They'll begin to take the bag off you and let you begin to fight *mar dh'ea* and they'll take the bag off you and let the hounds after the cat."

'"Very well so," says the poor man, "I'll do as you are saying."

'Home he came and the neighbour had the children

safe and sound before him. "Well, I brought you the
shoes," says he to the children, "but the shoemaker was
telling me that he couldn't make any shoes for you,"
says he to the cat, "until yourself come in to him and get
your measure taken. And he told me to bring you in to
him next Saturday."

'"That'll do so," says the cat.

'When Saturday came round, he got a fine big bag and
told the cat that the safest way for him to go in to Gort
was below in the bag and that no one would see him.
The cat agreed. So he put the cat into the bag and
started off for Gort.

'As soon as the bootmaker got the first chance, he
made off to the man that lived in the Big House and he
told him to have his horses and pack of hounds ready on
such a day and that as soon as he'd meet so-and-so coming into Gort, to take the bag off him and that he'd get a
big cat within in it and that he'd have the hunt of his life.
The Master of the Big House said that he'd have the
pack ready to meet him at the Blackwater near Ceann
na hAbhann.

'As soon as the poor man reached Ceann na
hAbhann, didn't the Master of the Big House pull his
horse across the road before him. "What have you in
that bag?" says he.

'"Isn't it all the damn same to you what I have in the
bag. That's my own business and you may go to hell,"
says the poor man.

'The Master of the Big House and his men grabbed
him and took the bag off him in spite of him. He tried to
put up a fight against them *mar dh'ea,* but he let the cat
go. They took the bag and shook it and out comes the
cat of a leap and headed towards the mountain. *As go
bráth* with the hounds hither after him and *as go bráth*
with the huntsmen hither after them. They never cried
crack until they landed in the mountain and one of the

hounds caught her before she reached home and when the rest of the pack came up, they tore the old witch of a cat to pieces — for she was nothing else!

'So they put down the kettle and made the tay and if they didn't live happy, that we may.'[3]

The story of *Rí na gCat* (The King of the Cats) is known the world over and many fine versions of it have been collected in Ireland too. The commonest Irish versions tell how a man, returning late one night from a fair, encountered a band of ferocious cats on a lonely mountain road. He was attacked by them and one cat seemed to be more vicious and more determined to kill him than all the rest. At last, he managed to catch this particular cat by the throat and squeezing with all his might, he choked the life out of it. He threw the dead cat from him on the road and started to make his getaway, but he had gone no more than a few steps when the cat which lay dead, as he thought, raised up its head from the ground and said — 'Tell so-and-so' (naming the man's mangy old cat that lay at home on the hearth) 'that *Rí-Chat Chruachain,* the King of the Cats is dead' — and then fell back dead again.

Some time later the man arrived home, tired and weary, and telling his wife about all that had happened to him, he mentioned at last the strange message that he had been asked to relay to their own old cat lying at his feet on the hearth. No sooner had he repeated his message than the old cat sprang to its feet, raced down the kitchen and, before leaping out over the half-door, turned and said, 'You took long enough to tell me the news!'

Most Irish versions of this story end there, but some offer a very macabre alternative ending which happens to have some interesting international ramifications, for instead of simply waltzing out and away, the mangy old cat sometimes shows no reaction whatsoever at the time to the message brought by the man of the house. Next morning, however, the man is found dead in bed with his throat cut from ear to ear and the old cat, having exacted its revenge for the death of the King of the Cats, gone never to be seen again.

Putting an end to this story and to their masters in such bloody fashion, it seems, is something that only Irish and Icelandic cats do and here we have an example of a direct connection between the Irish and the Scandinavian folk traditions, for nowhere else is this throat-cutting-in-revenge motif found except in Ireland and in Iceland. The Irish and the Icelanders have contacts stretching back in history for nearly a thousand years, of course, and it is nice to note another point of cultural contact, however small, between these two great cultures.

One of the many Irish versions of the King of the Cats was taken down in County Wexford by Patrick Kennedy more than one hundred and thirty years ago. He published it in his *Fireside Stories of Ireland* in 1870 under the title 'The Enchanted Cat of Bantry'.

'Long ago, after the English first came to Ireland, there were continual fights and scrimmages between themselves (their great strength was down in the baronies of Forth and Bargy), and the people in the upper part of the country, who would have no rulers except the old royal blood of Leinster, the O'Cavanaghs. Parties from each side would drive away cattle from their enemy, and kill the owners if they resisted. A little *bodach* of the English side that lived off towards Ballinvogga came in the dead of night with a boy of his to a lonesome house somewhere near the Glounthaan, killed the poor owner and some of his family, and drove away all the cattle that were in the place, and that was only a cow and a sheep. But mind, when they were getting home they found themselves pursued, and had no way to save their lives but by breaking into a chapel. I don't know whether it was the one at Rathgarogue or Temple Udigan.

'When the crowd went by, and they were relieved of their fright, they began to feel hungry. So they killed the sheep and were roasting a quarter of it at a fire they made out of old coffin boards, when a big cat with blazing eyes came in through the wall, and miawed out, "*Shone feol!*" (*Is uaim feoil,* flesh is from me, i.e. I want flesh). They were so frightened they gave him the quarter that was roasting. When he ate it he licked his chops and roared out again, "*Shone feol!*" and so on till he gobbled up all the sheep and three quarters of the cow. Hoping that he'd leave them a bit for themselves, they were boiling a piece of the beef over the fire in the cow's hide, stuck up on four stakes with some water in the hollow, but he bawled out more vicious that ever, when all the rest was down the red lane, "*Shone feol!*"

'Well, they gave him the piece that was simmering, and while he was *aten* it they got out and they were making the road home as fast as they could. They were not a quarter of a mile away when the moon happening to show her face, the *bodach's* boy cried out, "Master, master, the cat is sitting on the crupper behind you." He turned round and was so wild with fright and anger, that he pushed at his tormenter with his pike over his left shoulder and whether he was killed or not down to the ground he came. *Ovock!* in a moment you'd think all the cats from Blackstairs to Carrickbyrne were round them, and before they could look round, the boy and his horse were down, and the wild creatures tearing them limb from limb. The master set spurs to his horse while they were at their work, and never cried crack till he was inside his own bawn and the gate locked. He was more dead than alive when he got in, and couldn't tell what happened to him for ever so long. At last he began to give his wife an account of what happened, but when he came to the blow he made with pike and the tumble of the cat, a *kitten* only half a year old that was sitting on a boss screamed out, "Oh, you thief, did you kill my uncle?" and without another word she flew at his throat, and tore out a piece the size of her own head. If he hadn't gone on a murdering business, his wife wouldn't be a widow from that day to the last of her life.'[4]

First and Last

I spent Christmas Eve 1973 in the Blue Stack Mountains in County Donegal, in a townland called Crooveenananta, in a house called *Teach Eoghan Phádraig.* Every house had a name in this Gaeltacht area some twelve miles west of Ballybofey and only a stone's throw away from my own county, lying to the south and east across *Cruach Chonallach* and *Cruach Eoghanach,* at the mouth of Barnesmore. Dead generations of McAloons and Quinns and McHughs and McDermotts and Wards — the commonest surnames that were strung along the sides of this lonely mountain valley lying in the shadow of *An Chruach Ghorm* — the Blue Stack itself — are commemorated in these house names, in so far as they still exist, for this once populous valley, divided by the Reelin River, where wooden bridges once resounded to the clatter of dancing feet at Sunday evening dances, is now almost totally denuded of its people.

I was fortunate to catch a glimpse of what life was like there when, as a teenager interested in Irish, I began to pay sporadic visits to this wild mountain glen. A fairly high proportion of its residents were monoglot Irish speakers, their command of that language being all the better for their comparative lack of acquaintance with the other language, English, the language of commerce in neighbouring Ballybofey and Glenties, where Irish speakers were accustomed to being mocked and jeered by some of the local sophisticates. As one Blue Stack's man said, commenting on the way people stared when one spoke Irish in Glenties — *Shílfeá go raibh adharca ort* (You would think you had horns). The Irish of the Blue Stacks, as I say, was rich and beautiful and to a relative beginner like myself at the time, not always wholly intelligible. Even good Irish speakers, further down the valley of the Reelin, where it joins the Finn near the village of Brockagh, never failed to be impressed by its purity — *tá seanGhaeilg mhaith fá na Cruacha* (They speak fine old Irish in the Croaghs) — they would say in admiration. And so they did and plenty of it.

Teach Eoghan Phádraig, one of the many McAloon households, was located about half way up the glen and was the home at the time of three of the very best of this community of gifted Irish speakers, Pádraig Eoghan Phádraig, Conall Eoghan Phádraig and their sister Máire Eoghan Phádraig. All three were in or around ninety years of age, but, nevertheless, hale and hearty and remarkably spry and active for their age. They were all that remained at home of a long family of boys and girls scattered to the four ends of the earth. Pádraig and Máire are now dead, leaving Conall to end his days in nearby *Cruach an Airgid* (Silverhill) — *an baile is deise ainm in Éirinn* (the most congenially named place in Ireland) — as someone once said.

Their father, Eoghan Phádraig Mac an Luain, was a noted singer in a place famous for singers and songs; the famous Anna Nic an Luain, from whom no less than four hundred songs have been collected, was a near neighbour and the houses of the locality frequently hosted the brothers Doherty, Mìcí Simie and John Simie, musicians and tradition-bearers par excellence. I met both the Dohertys there at different times and saw with my own eyes the courtesy and the respect they were shown and the welcome they were given by one and all. Eoghan Phádraig Mac an Luain had passed on a great number of his songs to his sons and though Pádraig himself was no singer, God knows, he was happy and proud to be able to recite in a kind of monotonous drone, the words of dozens and dozens of his father's songs.

Pádraig told me that his father had once been taken away to Donegal Town some time about the turn of the century by a man called 'Lide' — as he pronounced it — who wrote down many of his songs, including a very unusual version of the Mermaid's Song — *An Mhaighdean Mhara*. This 'Lide' was, in fact, none other than Seosamh Laoide, a prominent Protestant Gaelic Leaguer of the time, and author of many books and articles on Donegal folklore.

The Harvest Fair in Glenties would see the Blue Stack's men celebrating there in strength and Pádraig Eoghan Phádraig told me how his father and his uncle once sat singing Irish songs in a Glenties pub, song after song, turn about, and as Pádraig put it, 'You wouldn't have found space to lay your finger on the counter before them, for every inch of it was covered with drinks' — all bought for them by a circle of appreciative listeners.

I paid many visits to *Teach Eoghan Phádraig* and was always made welcome there — two eggs and a mug of strong tea brewed on the clear coals of the open hearth fire were a sure testimony to the strength of that welcome and of their willingness to co-operate with me in the task of having their traditions recorded for posterity. Pádraig was the boss and he usually did the talking, his discourse interrupted now and then by Conall — never

55

by Máire — and then only when a word or line of a verse heard long ago had momentarily escaped his prodigious memory.

Following a bit of general chat about this and that, my adventures since I last visited there and how things were in the North — *'Caidé mar tá na Gaeil ins na Sé Chondae?'* (How are the Catholics in the Six Counties getting on?) — Pádraig would initiate the serious business of the evening by enquiring *'An bhfuil an ceamara leat an iarraidh seo?'* (Have you brought the camera?) — the 'camera' in this instance being my tape recorder. This was the signal that he was ready to begin recording and, from that on, the evening was given over to memories — songs and stories, proverbs, riddles and tongue twisters and accounts of long ago.

Christmas Eve 1973 was, as I say, only one of many magical evenings I spent by that humble fireside, exploring and discussing the cultural affairs of what was to all intents and purposes a dead world. Pádraig was himself quite well aware of the shrinking, crumbling context of the Gaelic world he grew up in and lived in all his days and he knew well the limited viability, out in the big bad world beyond the mountains, of the kind of cultural currency he and I were dealing in, for he once began to tease me about my constant anxiety to record the old songs and stories before it was too late, emphatically declaring that it was too late already, for didn't any fool know that according to the prophecy there was now only a decade or two left till the end of the world and where was the point in planning for posterity when there wasn't going to be any. Two thousand years, Pádraig said, the world was to last from the time of our Lord and sure wasn't the two thousand years already punched as near as made no difference! There was a catch, of course, as Pádraig went on to inform me with a chuckle — it wasn't two thousand years the world was supposed to last but two thousand years and a bit — and who was to say how long or how short the bit might be.

That Christmas Eve, Pádraig, I remember, began by describing and then performing a trick he called *Cleas na bPréataí* (The Potato Trick) — a kind of Spot the Lady with spuds, an illusion involving the counting out of potatoes, cap in hand, into various piles while keeping a single potato concealed in the cap all the while, dropping it and picking it up and generally baffling an audience desperately trying to keep track of what was happening. We talked of many other things that evening, including one of Pádraig's favourite subjects — Donegal's own saint, Colmcille.

Colmcille, it seems, wasn't much of a saint to begin with. In fact, as this story shows, he was severely lacking in charity, for which failing he duly got his come-uppance as you will shortly hear. He had a servant girl who was busy baking bread while Colm, as Pádraig generally referred to him, was outside watering the corn which was parched due to a very dry season. A beggarman entered the house looking for alms. Colmcille never gave alms to anyone, it seems, and the servant girl said that she had nothing to give him. She was kneading dough for the bread and she said that all she could give him was a bit of the dough. The beggarman took the dough and flung it down into the heart of the fire and out of the fire grew a bunch of green corn. The beggarman left and when Colm came in he saw the corn growing out of the fire and he knew immediately that it was no beggarman, but our Blessed Lord that had asked for alms and been refused. He ran after Him and caught up with Him and threw himself on his knees before Him begging for forgiveness. He actually tore the skin from his shins, so intense was his repentance. The skin was placed under a pot and later when the pot was lifted, all the rats and mice in the world ran out from underneath it.

Origins, the first of this and the first of that, have always exercised a tremendous fascination for the folk mind and explanations for all kinds of 'firsts' are as plentiful and as fanciful as could be. The Donegal explanation for the origin of rats and mice, stemming from St Colmcille's lack of charity, is matched by the following story, which not only gives the low-down on the origin of rats and mice, but throws in bonhams too for good measure. It is called 'How the first Bonhams, Rats and Mice came to be in it' and it was written down in 1937 in Kiltartan country by full-time collector Seán Ó Flanagáin.

'There was once a man and he was very rich. He had anything he wanted but he was on the look-out for an animal that would eat up all the vegetables that he'd have left over and he couldn't find any to do so. So this day, a holy man happened to go the way and he called into his house. He gave him something to eat and he was telling him how he had everything he needed, only if he had an animal that would eat up all the vegetables he had left over, he'd be satisfied.

'"Well, good man, if that's all that's troubling you," said the holy man, "I'll soon set that right. Have you got any lard in the house?"

'The man said he had and he got some. The holy man took some and he put it under a large washing tub on the floor and then he began to pray. After a time, he raised the tub up and out rushed a whole clutch of bonhams and the sow with them.

'"Now," said the holy man, "you have got something to eat up all the vegetables you can spare."

'Now there was a man within and he wanted to experiment on his own, so when he got their backs turned, he stole some of the lard and he took it home to his own house and put it in under another tub and began to pray, until he'd see what would happen. After a while, he raised up the tub and out ran a great crowd of rats and mice. That was what he had and so, that's how the first bonhams came to the country and the first rats and mice — the result of stealing. That's why the rats and mice will be rogues until the end of time. . .'[1]

The people of the Clare/Galway border area, where Seán Ó Flanagáin collected so much of his material, also directed their attention to manufacturing an explanation for the origin of goats. The answer is here, in a story called 'How the Devil Brought the First Goat to Ireland', noted down by Seán Ó Flanagáin in 1937:

'There was a poor man in it one time and it's what he used to be doing — gambling. There wasn't a shilling ever he earned that he didn't gamble again in the night and 'twas from one shilling to the next until in the heel of the hunt he had nothing left but the roof over his head and the four walls. He had everything lost except his religion and whatever way the world would go, he'd go to Mass anyway when Sunday would come around.

'This Saturday night, he was out all night and he had the last shilling he had in the world lost in the gambling and when he got up on Sunday morning he was feeling very *brónach* in himself. Anyways he started off for Mass and who would he meet on the road but the finest dressed gentleman he ever saw. "Jack," says he, "where are you going?"

'"Yerra, where would anybody be going of a Sunday morning but to Mass?" says Jack.

'"Sure you'll be time enough, Jack," says the stranger, "mightn't we as well have a game before you go anyway."

'"But, sure I haven't a stake in the world," says Jack.

'"Never mind," says the gentleman, pulling out a purseful of gold sovereigns, "sure I'll give you a stake." And he handed Jack a gold sovereign.'

'Well, they began to play and if ever they did, Jack began to win and he was winning ever and ever until the middle of Mass was over and then he began to lose and he was losing ever and ever until Mass was over and he had lost every penny. Then the gentleman began to grin and laugh. "Ha—ha, my boyo," says he to Jack, "I have won all back again and not only that but I have won your soul also as you didn't go to Mass when you should have. I am the devil from hell," says he, "and I'm taking you off with me now, down to hell."

'"O, musha, bad enough," says Jack, "and will you give me any chance at all? You know I have a poor mother at home to keep up," says he, "and maybe you could see your way to giving me a bit of a chance."

'"Well," says the devil, "I'll give you two chances — you must bring me an animal that I won't know and I'll bring you an animal and you must be able to know her name. I'll give you until such and such a time to do that," says he.

'The devil went on his way and Jack made for home. "Ara, ma'm, *a ghrá*," says he, "I'm swept, I'm whipped a cripple."

'"What's up with you, Jack, *a stóirín*," says the mother. Jack told her the whole story. "Oh, musha, bad enough, *a ghrá*," says she, "but we'll do our best anyways. Have you got long?"

'"I have until such a day," says he.

'Well, she started thinking of herself then how would they get an animal that the devil wouldn't know. At last she went out in the yard and she killed a goose, a duck and a hen. Then she got Jack to go and kill an old ass and an old cow that they had. She went then and got a barrel of tar and covered herself all over with tar and stuck on the feathers and quills of the goose, duck and hen, *trína chéile*. Then she went and put a pair of ass's ears on herself and a cow's tail, and when she was fully done up you never saw such a sight in all your born days.

'"Now, Jack," says she, "drive me out before you to where the devil is to meet you, but for your life, don't speak to me or call me any name." Off they started and they never cried halt till they came to the hill where the devil was to meet them. They halted there and, indeed, 'twasn't long till they saw the man making up at the foot of the hill and he driving an animal that they never saw the likes of before. "Listen," says the mother, "and see if you can hear him calling him by name." The two of them listened and it wasn't long till the strange animal made a spring up on the wall and in over it into a field. In went the man after him and he shouting, "Hurra *gabhar*, hurra *gabhar*."

'"By dad, Jack," says the mother, "that strange animal he has with him is called a goat and that's what you'll call him when he comes up."

'The devil came up and he driving the goat before him. "Good morrow, Jack," says he.

'"Good morrow kindly, sir," says Jack.

'"By dad, Jack," says the devil, "you have a strange animal with you."

'"Musha, I suppose, you know his name well, sir," says Jack. The devil looked the strange animal up and down, again and again, "He has ass's ears on him and a cow's tail but, damn it," says he, "he is neither an ass or a cow, for he is growing every sort of feathers — indeed, Jack," says the devil, "damn the bit of me knows what kind of an animal he is black, blue or white. By dad, Jack," says he, "you're a free man forever if you can tell me the name of this animal here that I have with me."

'"Yerra, sure man alive," says Jack, "isn't that an old goat, what else!"

'"You have me, Jack," says the devil. "I'll never bother or come near you any more and what's more I'll leave you the goat and you can keep her." Not long after that the goat had two kids and that's how the first goats came to Ireland. Jack and his mother put down the kettle and made the tay and if they didn't live happy, that we may.'[2]

The main body of Irish folk tradition concerning rats seems to be centred on the important business of being able to get rid of them. This could be done in several different ways — by the use of clay, for example, which was supposed to have the power of banishing rats when laid for them in very much the same way that one might lay ordinary rat poison. Clay from Old Drumragh graveyard, outside the town of Omagh, as well as clay from Tory Island (always to be lifted by one of the Doogan family) or elsewhere in Donegal, Gartan clay (always to be lifted by one of the O'Friels) also had this property and, in addition, it was said, this clay had the ability to prevent houses going on fire. John O'Donovan, writing in 1838, tells us that the clay from Inishglora off the west Mayo coast has the ability to kill frogs, rats and mice and preserves houses from burning and people from fever. Some clay! Other curious uses of clay are recorded in County Clare, where the clay from St Maccrithi's grave in Cillmhaccrithe was sometimes thrown against the wind to calm a storm, and in County Derry, where Banagher Sand, as it was called, from the tomb of St Muireadhach O'Heney, if thrown against an opponent in a law-suit was believed to secure judgement in favour of the thrower. It was supposed to be lifted by one of the O'Heneys for this purpose.

But, perhaps the commonest traditional method of getting rid of rats was that known as 'billeting'. This involved writing a letter to the rats intimating to them that they were most unwelcome where they were and advising them to betake themselves elsewhere. It was important when naming an alternative home for the rats to choose a place where they would never lack sustenance — a flour mill or the like — otherwise, if disappointed in their new billet, the rats were likely to return to their original lodgings, more vicious and voracious than ever before. The letter with the notice to quit was generally left on a pad frequented by the rats, somewhere where they would be sure to see it. An additional refinement was for the letter to be accompanied by a message couched in the form of a palindrome. 'Rats Live on No Evil Star' was one such formula designed to confer special additional powers on this communication.

The folklore manuscript collection at the Department of Irish Folklore, University College, Dublin, contains some fascinating material on this subject including the following copy of a letter written in 1944 by the former minister at Mosside Presbyterian Church, County Antrim to Miss Annie Irwin of Portballintrae in the same county:[3]

Dear Miss Irwin,

Minnie has just told me that you would like to have a full story of the flight of the rats from Mosside Manse and of the letter that was written to them. I can give you all this. It is clearly remembered by me.

It happened in the early autumn of 1899. Our servant, as you may remember, was Ruth ——. She had a sister named Maggie who came to spend a short holiday with her at the Manse. The Manse was infested with rats. Mrs —— and I used to hear them running about the hall about bed-time. As a matter of fact, I trapped and killed nine in one day in the pantry.

On the evening after Maggie came to stay with Ruth, she said to Mrs —— — 'Did you ever hear of writing a letter to rats telling them to leave a house and go to a house where they would get plenty?' Mrs —— replied, 'No, Maggie, I never did, but if you think it would do any good you should drop them a note to that effect.' So

Maggie got pen and paper and wrote the note — a respectful production — and placed it where they came out into the house — that was below the stairs in the hall.

My brother John came the next evening to spend a day or two with us and we told him about the rats and the letter. Curiosity led him to retrieve the letter and read it to us. He then restored it to where he got it. It was away in the morning and from that day until the day we left the Manse there was never a rat in the house. I forgot to mention that Maggie said that the letter to the rats must be written by a Roman Catholic (which she and Ruth were). The house she told them to go to was simply infested with them. I subjoin a copy of Maggie's letter every word of which I clearly remember.

Your old and loving friend —

Dear Rats,

Will you please leave the Manse altogether and go over to McAllister's. There is plenty of good meal there.

Yours Truly,
Maggie

Dead and Buried

Death is not a very cheerful subject, but any serious folklore collector will readily testify that it surely is one of the most popular topics of conversation you could find and death omens (such as the banshee), wake customs of all kinds, funerals (phantom and real), graves and graveyards, ghosts and apparitions are sure-fire lines of enquiry to follow when sounding out a new informant. Everyone, it seems, has something to say about some aspect of this subject.

In 1956, for example, Michael J. Murphy, full-time folklore collector with the former Irish Folklore Commission and still happily in harness with the Department of Irish Folklore at University College, Dublin, took down the following macabre piece of information from Daniel Gillan, aged eighty-nine, a farmer, of Losset, Cary, County Antrim:

'Like many another one, this woman had a child and it was spoiled. The child used strike the mother and she would never chastise it. The child took ill and died and when it was dead, its arm kept rising up and striking out.

'They sent for the doctor and he pronounced it dead. So they sent for the priest. He came and he sat down and he looked at the dead child. He watched the arm rise up and strike. He went outside and he called the mother of the child after him and he says:

'"The child in life was never reprimanded and now it's reprimanding you."

'And he commanded the mother to go and cut a bush — a broom or something — and to sit beside the dead child and every time the arm came up to strike she was to beat it till it quit. My father said that that woman — and you may imagine the state she was in beating her own dead child — that woman had to sit for half a day and a whole night and never leave the bedside. . . beating the arm of her dead child till it quit and was quiet. That is true. My father told it all.'[1]

Cáit Ní Bhrádaigh from County Longford, gives us this interesting list of death omens and death customs many of which were commonplace all over Ireland:[2]

If a cock crows after dusk it is a sign of death in the house.

Nine magpies seen together signify death in townland.

Four magpies seen together means a death in the house nearest to them.

If a picture falls in a house it signifies a death either in the house or among the immediate relatives.

If a hen crows in on the door there will be a death in the family very soon.

A rainbow over a house is a sign of death.

To dream of loss of an eye-tooth is a sure sign of a death.

If one is stooping and looking towards the ground when one hears the cuckoo for the first time it signifies a death before she comes again.

If a man riding a grey horse meets a funeral there will be another death in the same family in the near future.

To dream of cabbage is a sign of death.

'Death bell in the ear' is a sign that some poor soul is wanting a prayer.

When a coffin is lifted off chairs or stands these should be at once thrown down and left lying until the corpse is removed from the house.

When a corpse is carried out point an iron at the top of

the house round about to drive out the spirit.

It is very unlucky to wear anything new to a funeral.

A person meeting a funeral should always turn back and walk at least three steps with the funeral.

Snuff left over after the wake should be kept as it cures a headache.

In Longford we are told too that you should never wipe your boots in a graveyard, while in Galway it was said that if you lost something in a graveyard you should never look for it. In Wexford, to stumble or fall in a graveyard was taken as a sure sign that the date of your own death was not likely to be all that distant, while all over the country it was not deemed proper for a pregnant woman to come in contact with a corpse or to enter a graveyard. If a woman heavy with child were to stumble in a graveyard, her child, it was believed, would be born with a club foot, though this could be counteracted by throwing a handful of graveyard clay at the woman in question. In much the same way, a pregnant woman who had the presence of mind to bend and make a tear in the hem of her petticoat, if she happened to meet a hare, could prevent her child having a hare lip.

In many places it was the norm for a young married woman who died to be buried with her own people and not with her husband's people, the belief being that if the husband married again, it would not do to have the two wives buried near one another in the same grave. In Tuosist, County Kerry, when a man called Michael died, nobody called Michael was allowed to assist in digging his grave, while if a person, say, of the McCarthy family died in the same area, nobody bearing that surname but two men of different surnames were charged with digging the grave. In Tipperary, if a grave was opened by mistake, it was the custom to place a loaf of bread in it before it was refilled while, generally speaking, no grave is opened anywhere on New Year's day, since it was thought that if that were done, then a grave would have to be opened in that same graveyard every day for a whole year. Also practically everywhere in Ireland it was always considered desirable to have four men of the same family name shoulder the corpse on its way to the graveyard. In Listowel, I am told, when the coffin reaches the graveyard and is lowered into the grave someone makes the descent into the grave along with it in order to loosen the screws that hold down the coffin lid before the grave is filled in.

The curious spectacle of segregated aisles in churches with the men on one side and the women on the other — 'trousers' churches' as I have heard them called — is now almost a thing of the past. In some places, the notion of keeping the men and women apart was carried to the extreme of having separate men's and women's burying places. Carrickmore, in County Tyrone, has a graveyard called *Reilg na mBan* (The Women's Graveyard) which denies admission to two classes of individuals — namely, live women and dead men, and Inishmurray, off the Sligo coast, boasts a *Teampall na bhFear* and a *Teampall na mBan* (a men's and women's graveyard), while *Reilg Chiaráin* on Cape Clear off the coast of Cork, like most Irish graveyards, makes no such distinction, but offers instead the unique guarantee that anyone buried there will go straight to heaven.

After a funeral, the last man out of the graveyard was in danger of bringing the bad luck with him and not only could one sometimes observe a scramble for the gate on the way out, but in days gone by the unseemly spectacle of two funerals racing each other into the graveyard could often be seen, each one anxious not to be the last one in so as to avoid imposing on their deceased loved one the task of carrying the water and guarding the gate until the next funeral came along. Nor were fisticuffs at funerals entirely unknown either as this report from County Louth reveals:

'About half a mile to the north side of the pier in Clogherhead there is a rock with two small depressions in it. This is known as St Denis's Boat. The story goes that Denis was a hireling and was constantly getting into trouble for idleness. One day his master came upon him idle and in a listening attitude. He asked Denis what he was doing and Denis said that he was listening to the bells in Rome and told his master that if he put a hand on each of his shoulders and listened that he too would hear the bells. The master did likewise and heard the bells.

'Denis immediately became a favourite with his master who fitted him out with a crude boat and allowed him to set out for Rome. On the way, a storm arose and his boat was wrecked while he was on his knees praying. His body, however, floated back in a kneeling positon to a rock and was recovered by the natives of Clogherhead.

'At that time, the graveyard was in the townland since known as Killslaughter, because the people of that district and the people of Clogherhead fought for the body for burial! In the morning, two coffins were found in place of one and as it was not known which contained the body of St Denis, both were buried in Killslaughter and gave that name to the graveyard.'[3]

The burial of saints and sinners alike was seldom attended by bloodshed, however, though, in truth, blows were struck from time to time. Near Castlepollard, in County Westmeath, two doves, the symbols of peace, used to accompany corpses on their way for burial and elsewhere white butterflies were frequently observed on such occasions. A white butterfly was believed to represent the soul of the deceased and as such it was always treated with respect, even reverence as in County Mayo where its capture often gave rise to the recitation of the following simple prayer before its release: *Féileacán Dé, Féileacán Dé, Tabhair go Flaitheas mé* (Butterfly of God, Butterfly of God, Lead me to Heaven). My own grandfather, James Cassidy, returning by horse and trap from the graveyard where he had just buried his infant son, recalled how he was accompanied by a white butterfly which fluttered between the horse's ears all the way home, disappearing only on his arrival.

My aunt Annie, James Cassidy's eldest child, belongs to the generation of Irish people that grew up in an Ireland still dominated by the old ways. The unusual events associated with a Tyrone funeral of long ago, which she describes here, tell us a great deal about the attitudes of the different religious denominations towards each other in that part of the world, without revealing, I am glad to say, any of the familiar northern bitterness. Annie was told this story by her uncle, Brian Slevin:

'I remember hearing Brian telling this story — somebody told it to him. It was some church anyway, but there was a funeral. And there was this wee man — a Catholic man — and he went to the wake. And at that time, away years ago, the morning of the funeral, the man of the house, he'd have two or three men go round with a bottle of whiskey and a glass to treat every man that went to the funeral.

'So this wee man got enough, he got a wee drop too much anyway and he went to the church and when the service was over, didn't he fall asleep with the drink from the night before and all. Nobody in the church seen him — he was in the seat but he fell down and he was sleeping.

'It was very late on that night when he wakened and come till himself and realised where he was. So he couldn't get out — it seems they locked up and he had no way of getting out. So the only thing he could think of was to ring the bell. So he started to ring the bell in the Protestant church the same night as the night of the funeral. And, of course, the neighbours heard it and the minister heard it and they come and they took fear and they wouldn't go in. The minister wouldn't venture in, do you see, for the bell had been tingling and ringing, and neither would the men. So it gathered up before all was over that there was a right crowd of people gathered to know what had happened. So they decided anyway that they would go for the parish priest.

'The parish priest landed anyway, got up out of his bed and landed, and he had a — now, whether he had a car, now, or a side-car — but he had a big rug with him and whether he put it around his shoulders or what, they were that excited they never noticed. So the priest opened the church door and he went in. He walked in and seen his man and knowed him so well and he had a wee chat with him inside. The man told him the whole story: "I was at the wake," says he, "last night and I got a lot of drink. I got more this morning," he says, "and when I went into the church I fell asleep."

'"Well," says the priest, "just keep quiet and we'll make a good thing out of this." So he got this big hairy rug. "Now," says the priest, "I want you to walk bent over like this and I'm putting this rug over your head, right over your head. Now, you do what I bid you and walk in the front and I'll go behind you. And I'll go out now and I'll tell the boys that he's here all right!" That was the devil — but it was only a Catholic man.

'He went out and he says to the minister, "I'll tell you what you'll do. Go on every side, make a path in the middle, you men, now. Keep on each side," he says, "I'm taking him out now — I'm putting him out."

'In he goes and he warned him to be sure and bend down and walk very low, just bend and crawl along and the rug was right out over his head. And he got behind him and your man walked out of the church door and up the path. Well, he said that they fainted in all directions. Some of them fainted and some of them run. They run in all directions when they seen what was coming out of the church. They thought it was the devil and instead of that it was a Catholic man the worse of drink!'

From far away to the south and in contrast to this northern story, here is an eerie account of the extra-ordinary facts behind the traditional burial practice of the Cantillon family in County Kerry.

'The ancient burial-place of the Cantillon family was on an island in Ballyheigh Bay. This island was situated at no great distance from the shore, and at a remote period was overflowed in one of the incroachments which the Atlantic has made on that part of the coast of Kerry. The fishermen declare they have often seen the ruined walls of an old chapel beneath them in the water, as they sailed over the clear green sea, of a sunny after-noon. However this may be, it is well known that the Cantillons were, like most other Irish families, strongly attached to their ancient burial-place; and this attach-ment led to the custom, when any of the family died, of carrying the corpse to the sea side, where the coffin was left on the shore within reach of the tide. In the morning, it had disappeared, being, as was traditionally believed, conveyed away by the ancestors of the deceased to their family tomb.'

'Connor Crowe, a County Clare man, was related to the Cantillons by marriage. "Connor Mac in Cruagh, of the seven quarters of Breintragh", as he was commonly called, and a proud man he was of the name. Connor, be it known, would drink a quart of salt water, for its medicinal virtues, before breakfast; and for the same reason, I suppose, double that quantity of raw whiskey between breakfast and night, which last he did with as little inconvenience to himself as any man in the barony of Moyferta; and were I to add Clanderalaw and Ibrickan, I don't think I should say wrong.

'On the death of Florence Cantillon, Connor Crowe was determined to satisfy himself about the truth of this story about the old church under the sea: so when he heard the news of the old fellow's death, away with him to Ardfert, where Flory was laid out in high style, and a beautiful corpse he made.

'Flory had been as jolly and as rollocking a boy in his day as ever was stretched, and his wake was in every respect worthy of him. There was all kind of entertainment and all sorts of diversion at it, and no less than three girls got husbands there — more luck to them. Everything was as it should be: all that side of the country, from Dingle to Tarbert, was at the funeral. The Keen was sung long and bitterly; and according to the family custom, the coffin was carried to Ballyheigh strand, where it was laid upon the shore with a prayer for the repose of the dead.

'The mourners departed, one group after another, and at last Connor Crowe was left alone: he then pulled out his whiskey bottle, his drop of comfort as he called it, which he required, being in grief; and down he sat upon a big stone that was sheltered by a projecting rock, and partly concealed from view, to await with patience the appearance of the ghostly undertakers.

'The evening came on mild and beautiful: he whistled an old air which he had heard in his childhood, hoping to keep idle fears out of his head; but the wild strain of that melody brought a thousand recollections with it, which only made the twilight appear more pensive.

'"If 'twas near the gloomy tower of Dunmore in my own sweet county, I was," said Connor Crowe, with a sigh, "one might well believe the prisoners, who were murdered long ago there in the vaults under the castle,

73

would be the hands to carry off the coffin out of envy, for never a one of them was buried decently, nor had as much as a coffin amongst them all. 'Tis often, sure enough, I have heard lamentations and great mourning coming from the vaults of Dunmore Castle: but," continued he, after fondly pressing his lips to the mouth of his companion, and silent comforter, the whiskey bottle, "didn't I know all the time well enough, 'twas the dismal sounding waves working through the cliffs and hollows of the rocks and fretting themselves to foam. Oh then, Dunmore Castle, it is you that are the gloomy-looking tower on a gloomy day, with the gloomy hills behind you; when one has gloomy thoughts on their heart, and sees you like a ghost rising out of the smoke made by the kelp burners on the strand, there is, the Lord save us! as fearful a look about you as about the Blue Man's Lake at midnight. Well then, anyhow," said Connor, after a pause, "is it not a blessed night, though surely the moon looks mighty pale in the face? St Senan himself between us and all kinds of harm."

'It was, in truth, a lovely moonlight night; nothing was to be seen around but the dark rocks, and the white pebbly beach, upon which the sea broke with a hoarse and melancholy murmur. Connor, notwithstanding his frequent draughts, felt rather queerish, and almost began to repent his curiosity. It was certainly a solemn night to behold the black coffin resting upon the white strand. His imagination gradually converted the deep moaning of old ocean into a mournful wail for the dead, and from the shadowy recesses of the rocks he imaged forth strange and visionary forms.

'As the night advanced, Connor became weary with watching; he caught himself more than once in the fact of nodding, when suddenly giving his head a shake, he would look towards the black coffin. But the narrow house of death remained unmoved before him.

'It was long past midnight, and the moon was sinking into the sea, when he heard the sound of many voices, which gradually became stronger, above the heavy and monotonous roll of the sea: he listened, and presently could distinguish a Keen, of exquisite sweetness, the note of which rose and fell with the heaving of the waves, whose deep murmur mingled with and supported the strain.

'The Keen grew louder and louder, and seemed to approach the beach, and then fell into a low plaintive wail. As it ended, Connor beheld a number of strange, and in the dim light, mysterious-looking figures, emerge from the sea, and surround the coffin, which they prepared to launch into the water.

'"This comes of marrying with the creatures of earth," said one of the figures, in a clear, yet hollow tone. "True," replied another, with a voice still more fearful, "our king would never have commanded his gnawing white-toothed waves to devour the rocky roots of the island cemetery, had not his daughter, Durfulla, been buried there by her mortal husband!"

'"But the time will come,," said a third, bending over the coffin,

　　　"When mortal eye — our work shall spy,
　　　And mortal ear — our dirge shall hear."

'"Then," said a fourth, "our burial of the Cantillons is at an end for ever!"

'As this was spoken, the coffin was borne from the beach by a retiring wave, and the company of sea people prepared to follow it; but at the moment, one chanced to discover Connor Crowe, as fixed with wonder and as motionless with fear as the stone on which he sat.

'"The time is come," cried the unearthly being, "the time is come; a human eye looks on the forms of ocean, a human ear has heard their voices: farewell to the Cantillons; the sons of the sea are no longer doomed to bury the dust of the earth!"

'One after the other turned slowly round, and regarded Connor Crowe, who still remained as if bound by a spell. Again arose their funeral song; and on the next wave they followed the coffin. The sound of the lamentation died away and at length nothing was heard but the rush of waters. The coffin and the train of sea people sank over the old church-yard, and never, since the funeral of old Flory Cantillon, have any of the family been carried to the strand of Ballyheigh, for conveyance to their rightful burial-place, beneath the waves of the Atlantic.'[4]

Begging their Bit

A bare generation or two ago, the highways and byways of Ireland were crowded with all kinds of wanderers — tramps, beggarmen, tinkers, *siúlóirí* (shoolers), packmen, hawkers and pedlars. In days gone by, every district had its own regular band of visitors — most of them welcome visitors, as we learn from this account taken down in 1955 from Alex Monaghan, aged seventy-three, of Belnaleck, County Fermanagh by the late Alex McConnell, also of Belnaleck, a much valued question-naire correspondent with the former Irish Folklore Commission and latterly the Department of Irish Folklore at University College, Dublin.

'Beggars in the old days were not at all looked down on as they are now. You see, they were very useful in their own way. In the first place, they were the only source of news the people had, I mean the country people. . . No one would ever turn out a beggar. He got a bundle of straw in the kitchen at night and some alms on his departure in the morning. They delivered messages for the people, sometimes over two or three counties. If they themselves were not going to a particular house, they knew another beggar who was and so passed on the message. Messages were sent from this part of the country as far as Dungannon, some fifty miles away. Possibly messages were delivered even further than that, but I knew my Granny sent a message to her brother from here to Dungannon in this way. They brought news and delivered news and kept the people in touch over a large area. Most of them were honest and would not steal on any account.

'Some of these wanderers were very independent and would just give you a bit of their mind if they were annoyed. One such character was Jemmy Meala as he called himself. It was in my Granny's time. He was a crabbed old fellow. He said he was away in his young days fighting in "furrin" parts and he used to go through all sorts of manoeuvres with his stick as a gun. One day, he called at the house of one Hughie G——, a rather mean sort of fellow who didn't at all relish the idea of giving a beggarman such a big feed as his wife (who was a big-hearted woman) had laid before Meala. Hughie G—— passed some remark about there being so many mouths to be filled (he had nine or ten children) and it annoyed Meala. So here is the grace before meals which Meala said on this occasion:

> Some have meat and wouldn't eat,
> And some would eat if they had it;
> Well, I have meat and I will eat,
> And the devil thank Hughie G—— for it!

'Having eaten, he looked at old Hughie and, says he, "Do you know, Hughie, what your name (G——) means?"

'"No," says Hughie.

'"Well," says he, "it means a low little mean little servant of God!"

'He never went back to that house. Old people to the present day will buy from every pedlar, gipsy or beggar and would consider it uncharitable if they did not.'[1]

Some of the sayings of another 'independent' beggarman who used to frequent parts of County Sligo were taken down in 1931 by Bríd Ní Ghamhnáin of Ballindoon, on the shores of Lough Arrow:

'There was, at one time, an old tramp called Terry the Grunter who used to wander round these parts often times. He lived principally on his wits and he composed satires about people who did not please him. He happened to be in Sligo when a certain solicitor died and he asked some of this man's brother solicitors for help. They refused him. When the funeral was starting, four solicitors carried the coffin part of the way to the cemetery. Terry the Grunter gave the following description of the affair:

There's a knave overhead and four underneath,
The body is dead and the soul on a journey,
The devil is at law and he wants an attorney.

'When the Protestant church at Riverstown was being built, the Bishop of Elphin came to consecrate it. He met our hero who, as usual, was on the look-out for money. The bishop refused him and the tramp wrote the following:

An English bishop came from Elphin,
To consecrate the church at Cooper Hill;
But if the devil himself came up from hell,
He would do it fully as well![2]

It may well be that the respect shown by country people to tramps and beggarmen in bygone days was due in some measure to their fear of being satirised by them in this fashion just as they feared the effects of the beggar's curse. Even the very threat of a curse could bring results, a trick often used by a certain Tipperary beggarwoman by the name of Máirín Raindí. She was always accompanied by her little daughter who used to sing out, in Irish, as they went from door to door — *Éinne a thabharfaidh déirce dúinn, go n-arda Dia suas ins na Flaithis é; agus éinne ná tabharfaidh, go n-arda Dia suas ins na Flaithis é —— agus go bplaba Sé anuas arís é!* (Anyone who gives us alms, may God raise him up to Heaven; and anyone who doesn't, may God raise him up to Heaven — and then slap him down again!)'[3]

To be able to resort to cursing, or to satire, was a handy stand-by when all else failed, though, it was, of course, an admission of failure — better by far to dazzle the opposition where possible by cunning strategem and clever use of one's wits, as did a certain spalpeen in a story collected in 1937 by full-time collector, Seán Ó Flanagáin. The storyteller, Mícheál Ó Murchú, aged sixty-six, then living in Kiltartan country, was a native of Clonmel, County Tipperary. His story is called 'How the Spalpeen got his Breakfast'.

'There was an old farmer in it one day and he had a five acre field of hay to cut and he took out the scythe in the morning about five o'clock and he was edging it and scratching his head at the same time. Begor, what steps up but a fine able-bodied man. He looked out at him and he going along the road.

'"Well, by gob," he says, "'tis an awful thing to see a fine able-bodied man like you walking along the road and a poor old man like me here in this five acre field trying to cut it."

'"Why, man," he says, "isn't I mad looking for work!"

'"Well," he says, "it was God sent you."

'In he goes, in over the ditch. He caught the scythe and he looked at it. "Ah, my man," he says, "that scythe is too near me." By gor, the poor farmer had to go home and get the hammer and bring it back till he'd untackle the scythe. . . and put it together again. He caught it and he looked at it. "Ah, 'tis too near me," he says, "all the time." By gor, he had to open it again and he tackled it up again.

'By gor, between times, he was called home to his breakfast. When he went in, there was a big cake of oaten bread made to him and a big mug of tea, a pound of butter and three eggs. He got a hold of the cake. . . and he gave it a clout of his hand and he made two of it — halved it, you know. Well, he caught the knife and he stuck it in the pound of butter and he took half of it.

'Well, the women of the house was walking around and, "Oh, Lord!" she says, when she seen what he had done. The lad never minded anything — he ate it and when he had that ate, he wheeled round and he caught the other half. "Are you there, Ma'am?" he says. "Oh, I am, Sir," she says. "Well, here is another 'Oh, Lord!' for you now," says he, making at the other half of the cake. By gor, he ate it and ate the three eggs and drank another mug of tea and walked out, himself and the farmer.

'And the farmer was to go to town when he got the mower. . . "Well," says the farmer to him, "do you think now," he says, "is that scythe too near you now?"

'"Musha, my dear man," he says, "do you see that big wood," he says, "that's out there, three mile away."

'"I do," says the farmer.

'"Well," says the spalpeen, "if it was that far from me, it would be too near me! Good morning, my man!"[4]

From a little further south — Kilgarvan, County Kerry — we hear of a beggarman whose intentions were every bit as dishonourable, but whose tactics were somewhat more obvious, though none the less effective for all that:

'There was another old beggarman with a fine white whisker, staying at a house in Gortlouchra, south-east of Kilgarvan. He kept his eyes continually on a pig's cheek which hung from a joist above him in the kitchen, and as he did so, he kept rubbing down his splendid whisker and saying, "You'll be off in the morning, or perhaps, before morning!" He meant the pig's cheek, but the woman of the house thought he was referring to the whisker. She began to advise him to leave it growing as it was, and not to cut it off, by any means.

'She made him a comfortable bed and felt satisfied. . . when he lay down with his whisker uncut or unshaven. But when she woke up the following morning, there was no trace to be seen of the whisker, the beggarman — or the pig's cheek!"[5]

International Tale Type 1544 — 'The Man Who Got a Night's Lodgings' is found in most European countries and, indeed, much farther afield, in places such as Turkey, India and the West Indies as well. In Ireland, it usually goes under the name 'Seán, Bí-i-do-Shuí!' or, in English versions 'Paddy, Eat-a-Bit!' Here is a fine version under the latter title, taken down from the late William Rourke, a native of Clonkeen, County Roscommon, by full-time collector James G. Delaney.

'This tailor was working in this house and the men of the house, like us here now, they were. . . talking about people that wouldn't ask people to eat. . . if they went in "rambling", they'd give them nothing. . . "They're there below," says this man, "our next door neighbours, they'd never ask no one. . . had they a mouth on them, to eat a bit."

'"I bet you my week's wages," says the tailor, "if you tell me when they're eating their breakfast tomorrow," he says, "they'll tell me eat," says he to the man of the house he was working with. He said he'd bet two week's wages with him and he did. Two week's wages. Whatever the tailor was getting a week for sewing, I don't know that, but he bet it.

'So he went down at the time they said anyhow and they were at their breakfast and he knocked and the man got up from the table — opened the door — and he let him in and the tailor says, "God bless the work!". . .

'"You, too," says the man. "And," he says, "is it any harm. . . to ask you, my good man, what's your name?"

'"Well, not one bit, Sir," he says, "my name is Paddy Eat-a-Bit."

'"Paddy Eat-a-Bit? Paddy Eat-a-Bit?" says he.

'"And I will and welcome," says the tailor.

'And you know, he didn't want it at all, but the man he bet with was outside the back door listening. And he got in and the woman says to him, "Well, we never know the taste of any of our neighbour's food," she says. "No matter what taste is on it, this is very good," he says, to let the man outside know he was eating, "the best I ate yet!"

'And ate a good feed of it: And he won the bet, won the bet. That's all that was in it.'[6]

James G. Delaney has been engaged in collecting folklore over a number of years in a good many corners of this island, not least in his own native Wexford, where he took down this account of local tramps of long ago from Walter Furlong of Grange Upper in the parish of Rathnure:

'Mrs Whalen up the lane here, had a special loft over the cowhouse for the tramps. They used to come over the mountains from Carlow and she give them lodgings and their supper and breakfast in the morning and a few pence. They'd come on a Saturday night and stay till

Monday morning. The lane would be black with them and you'd want a bag of pennies for the callers on a Monday morning.

'I often saw four or five of them making up the lane on a Saturday night and they going like blazes for fear they'd be too late. She had three or four beds for them. Any of them that would be late, she'd have to make a special shake-down for them on the boards. They'd be hurrying to get a bed.

'Simon the Streel used to be one of the tramps about the district. His clothes used to be in tatters and the pieces flying out of him. That's the reason he was called 'the Streel'. He said he was descended from the Kings of Leinster. He came from the County Kildare and he allowed that his ancestors lived in Tara. He said that they conquered the O'Rourkes of Breffni and the Maguires of Fermanagh and they were bosses of the whole country. He said that there were four Popes at his mother's Office! He used to be around Grange and Rathnure all the time.

'Jack Dooley used to be taking yarns out of Simon. Anyone that'd be telling yarns, Jack would say to them, "You're as big a liar as Simon the Streel — he said that there were four Popes at his mother's Office." Simon generally stopped at Whalens. Dooley asked Simon what his father was remarkable for. Simon said that they could not carry arms in his father's time but his father was noted for being a good hand at pelting stones. There wasn't any man with a rifle had as good a shot as his father had with a stone, Simon said. Dooley used to be working at Whalens and he used to be annoyed with the tramps. He often threatened to burn the house over them.

'Bridgid Whalen would go out on a Sunday morning to see would any of them be going to Mass. "I wasn't at Mass this seven year," one of them would say, "and it's

not worth my while going now." Another would say —
"Sunday is a day of rest — the chapel is too far away."
Mrs Whalen used to give them copies of *The Homeless
Child* to read. It was all about poor people and about
giving charity to them and looking after their wants.

'I was over in Redmonds of Ballybawn, one night,
and an old fellow come in. It was a terrible night with
storm and rain. It was Paddy from Nash — a well-known
tramp in the neighbourhood. He asked could he be let
stay the night. Mrs Redmond said she'd make up a bed
for him in the stable loft, the night was so hard.

'About half an hour afterwards, this other poor man
come to the door and it was spilling twice as bad. He
asked to stop and said he had been refused in several
places and that that house was his last hope. She said she
had no room, that she had one already and couldn't
accommodate the second. I said that perhaps the two of
them would sleep together. I asked Paddy would he
sleep with the other man in one bed. "Well," says he,
"I'd like to see the man" and he shouted to the man at
the door — "Come in, my poor man, and we'll have a
look at you."

'The other came in. He was a fine big tall man and the
rain was dripping out of him. So he looked in the corner
and he spotted Paddy. "In the name of the good God
Almighty," he says, "sure it can't be Paddy from Nash is
here! Well, I'm thankful to you ma'am," says he to Mrs
Redmond, "for offering me the shelter, but I'd rather be
caught dead in the ditch, than sleep with that hangman,"
he says. "I'd rather be got dead in the ditch than sleep
with unfortunate Paddy from Nash, that low mane outlaw!" And off he went out the door again.'[7]

Whatever offence poor Paddy from Nash may have
been guilty of in the eyes of his fellow beggarman will
probably never be known now, but the pride which prevented the desperate late-comer from sharing a bed with

him is a feature often commented upon as being common among tramps, some of whom, like 'Simon the Streel' were even wont to go as far as to make no secret of their noble origins — all of which added to the air of mystery that surrounded their personalities and their various comings and goings. A wary suspicion of them too was probably never very far from the minds of the country people who received them in their homes — at least, something akin to that is revealed in an account, which I recorded from Annie O'Hagan of Eskra, County Tyrone, of an incident involving the evil eye or 'blinking', as northerners call it:

'You know, there was such a thing as people "blinking" things away back, years ago. I heard tell of a man, now, and he was ploughing. And this boy — he was kind of on a begging line — come to the street anyway and your man was coming with his horses. The beggarman says — "You have a pair of fine horses, especially one — he's a great horse, that."

'Your man put in his horses to feed them till he'd get his dinner and when he went out to give them a drink, his best horse — the horse that the beggarman looked at — was down in the stable, kicking. And he knowed, there and then, from the remarks that the beggarman had passed that there was something wrong. And the cure was, if you burn some of their clothing, it breaks the charm that they have. And he had no hesitation; he ran into the house as quick as he could and the first thing he got his hands on was a butcher knife and he down the lane after this boyo.

'And the beggarman looked round and he called to him to stop — "If you don't stop," says he, "I'll cut your throat! Stand your ground!" And he took the tail of his coat and, there and then, he just boned a lump off the tail of the coat. And he back with it and he took a match and he lit the coat, he lit it in front of the horse. And just when the thing was burnt out, up jumped the horse and started his feeding. And the horse was dying before that.

'I don't know whether the beggarman knowed he was doing this to the horse or not, but he passed the remark, do you see, to this fellow about the horses — "especially one" he says. They called it "blinking". In them years, away back, God bless us, sure it was awful. It was awful. You couldn't have anything with them."

The late Séamus Ó Duilearga and also Seán Ó Súilleabháin, the two great pioneers of Irish folklore in modern times, both radiating enormous zeal and enthusiasm for the task of collecting Irish folk tradition in all its many forms, managed to rally support from many quarters for their campaign, largely carried out under the auspices of the former Irish Folklore Commission, which was established in 1935. Among the many voluntary contributors to the Commission's holdings was the late Rodney Green, former Director of the Institute of Irish Studies at Queen's University, Belfast, who, as a young man, made some excellent collections in counties Antrim and Down. Here is an account of tramps and travellers of one kind or another which he took down in 1943 from Mrs Mary Ann Taggart, aged seventy-eight, then living in Magheragall, County Antrim and a native of Mullaghcarter in the same county:

'Magennis come round early every week. He had everything from a pin till combs, brushes. . . thread. Henry Briggs carried a pack. . . and sold shirts and trousers. It was more linen shirts, towels and handkerchiefs that Basil Make sold. . . Henry McCann had a perambulator with things in it that he sold. We used to meet James Low coming home from school. "I'll give you a wee handkerchief," he'd say. "Can you spell woody t'ruffy?" "WOO-WDY-PHTH-RUFFY." "Can

you spell Constantinopley?" "CON-STANT-INOPTLE."
"Can you spell Aurora Borealis?" "AURORI BORE-
ALIS." He'd ask you to spell the King of the Jews in
syllables —

> A clout and a clod spells Nebby o' Nod,
> A knife and a razor spells Nebby o' Nazur,
> A thimble and a ring spells o' Nazur the king,
> An old pair of slippers and a new pair of shoes,
> Spells Nebby o' Nazur, the King of the Jews.

'He went into the schools and asked the master to let
him question them. He'd give them wee presents. He
sold shirts, towels, underclothes and things like that. He
had a big pack. They had oilcloth packs with a strap on
them and threw them over their shoulders. They put
their arm through it and swung it. The stuff they sold
was got from big shops in Belfast, Lurgan and Lisburn.
It was just "reddin-outs' and things that was spoiled.

'There was an old fellow went round with a wee donkey's cart, crying "rags, ropes and bones". He carried a
box of sweets for the childer and he got them for a
"lock" of sweets. Praying Mary was a wee old woman.
She came in and sang hymns and then she got a drop of
tea. Anne Crossey used to be always talking about
having a weakness in her legs. She was drunk — that's
what was wrong with her. Then there was Darkie Jen-
kins and Bess Stonefield and Eliza Green. Annie Tippin
of Moira carried the post and then begged after that.
Then there was John Thomson — "John Thomson's
news" was a by-word for anything that was three years
old.

'There'd be as many as two or three in a day, coming
round. They begged a bowlful of flour or tea or potatoes
— then when they got it, they sold it at night to somebody that had pigs.

'"Tipperary" — John Bell was his right name — was

fond of children and sang songs. He would have recited any prayer, Roman Catholic or ours, for a penny. After the wife died, he lost his mind. He always stayed at night in a haystack. . . He died in Lurgan Union. George Brown was a darkie. He went barefoot, summer and winter, and he had just a bag threw round his shoulders for a coat. There was an old man we called "Monday" — he always come round that day. There was things he used always to say — "I gave the Queen my best days, she gave me the hard road", "There's a slate off — it's jingling", "If you've no coppers, silver'll do".

'Pat Green saved Commodore Watson's life once. The Commodore was riding himself at some race at Antrim. Pat overheard them making a plot to throw him coming home and he went to the Commodore and he says, "Gawney, they're plotting to kill you, master."

'"Get up beside me," says the Commodore, "they'll kill you for telling me this."

'"They'll never think of me," says Pat. He took his chance among the crowd.

'The Commodore used to always give him money. One Sunday morning, when the Commodore was going to church, he gave him something. Pat went round and met him again. "Gawney, master, we've met again," says Pat.

'He stole a pair of boots, once but they were too wee for him. He took them back to the shop and, says he — "They're too wee for Pat's big feet."[8]

'There was fish-men from the Loughshore come round with the donkey and cart selling pollans and terch. McAtamley and McAlinden was the turf men I mind coming round here. They were from the Montiaghs. There was herring men too. They used to call — "Fresh herrings, all alive," and the people would have shouted back — "Three stinking out of five." There was women went round with salt herrings in cans. You'd get a dozen for eightpence or ninepence. **A shilling was counted dear.'⁹**

Tea

Tea originated in China nearly five thousand years ago, give or take a century or two. Chinese tradition credits the Emperor Chinnung — to whom all agricultural and medical knowledge is traced — with the discovery of the virtues of tea, in or around the year 2737 BC, though it is also claimed that a knowledge of tea travelled eastward to China having been introduced there by an ascetic missionary from India. Still other accounts say that the advent of tea may have simply come about through the necessity of boiling drinking water for health reasons.

Whatever about all that, it seems that from China, a knowledge of tea was carried into Japan about the year 800 AD and the Japanese subsequently developed an elaborate tea-serving ceremony of social and religious significance. It is somewhat odd that, although many of the products of China were known and used in Europe in early times, no mention of tea is made in Europe — not even by Marco Polo — until about four hundred years ago. The first consignment of it is said to have reached Holland about the year 1610 and some fifty years later we hear of its introduction to England by a London coffee house proprietor, one Thomas Garraway. A little earlier, in the year 1615, we find what is probably the earliest reference to tea in the English language in a letter from a Mr Wickham, an agent of the East India Company, who when writing to a colleague from Japan makes mention of 'a pot of the best sort of chaw'. Samuel Pepys mentions that on 25 September 1660, he 'did send for a cup of tea, a China drink of which I never had drunk before.'

Tea is drunk all over the world today and countries such as Sri Lanka, Japan, Kenya, Uganda, Mozambique, Tanzania and the USSR have joined India and China as leading tea producers while of all the tea-drinking countries, Ireland has the greatest per head per day consumption of this commodity.

Such was not always the case, however, and Michael Corduff of Rossport, County Mayo, writing in 1941 and describing popular attitudes towards tea (and coffee) in his native place, reveals a situation which also held true for many other parts of the western seaboard of Ireland. He writes as follows:

'In this part of Erris tea was practically unknown among the people up to 1870 and as late as 1885 or perhaps some years later many households did not use tea. But gradually the use of tea was growing and becoming more widespread until people acquired much taste for it and secured the reputation of being the greatest tea drinkers in Ireland.

'Before the introduction of tea in Erris, coffee was a well-known beverage with the people from earlier times when it was imported along the coast by smuggling vessels. Even after tea became known people used coffee in preference down to a late period and some of the very old people today, say those of ninety years or so, prefer coffee to tea, as they drank coffee at an early age, long before they ever tasted tea. The importing smugglers had their agents along the coast for the sale and distribution of coffee just the same as tobacco.

'Formerly people concocted a beverage somewhat like tea from a plant known as *Tae Mór* which used to grow in the meadows of rich soil. The plants were cut from the ground and tied up into small bundles and hung up to dry in the house. When dried, its leaves and seeds were rubbed between the hands and a mixture resembling tea was obtained. This was boiled or stewed and the juice with some milk added was then drunk. The effusion thus produced from the native vegetable plant had a taste and a colour resembling tea and after drinking it a person felt its stimulating and exhilarating effect. Some people had developed a great liking for this beverage but with the more extended use of tea the native product gradually fell into disuse and ultimate abolition.'[1]

Naturally, enough, inland parts of Ireland were not in a position to benefit to the same extent from the smuggling trade and so coffee was unknown there and tea wasn't all that common either. Recently, my aunt, Annie O'Hagan, described for me how her grandmother (a native of the Carleton country of County Tyrone) first got a taste for tea. Her father was dead set against it and only the action of an itinerant shoemaker called Scallon, who happened to be making shoes for the family at the time, was sufficient to save her from her father's wrath. Here's how Annie put it:

'There'd only be tea at Christmas, do you see. That would be a very set time they would get it. There'd come two ounces of tea into the house for Christmas, two ounces, now. That's when it come first. You got tea once at Christmas — that was the feast. And that was left past, the remainder of the tea was stuck in behind the ribs of the house and it would never be introduced again till Easter. When Easter come, they got another cup of tea and that was it finished then till Christmas again!

'Grandma was a lump of a girl, she had to work brave and hard — milking cows and all the rest — and she got the taste and her mother knew she was at this. Her father was very, very strict in one way and then he'd make a fool of himself when he'd go to the town — he'd drink and buy drink till the cows would come home — but he didn't allow tea in the house. Grandma said till her mother one day — Scallon was making the shoes at the time — that she would like a wee drop of tea. "Well," says she, "I'll tell you what you'll do. Get the shovel and take a *lock* of clear coals down and put them under the bed and get your wee tin and put it on the clear coals."

'Well, at that time, whatever way tea was, you could smell the tea a-making at the road. So she was at this for a right wee while, making tea under the bed and one morning your man come in, her father come in and he smelled the tea — he found this peculiar smell and he knew it was bound to be the smell of tea somewhere. He searched and on he went — and, of course, the smell got stronger as he got nearer — he went down anyway and he got the tin under the bed.

'So Scallon was in the corner making the shoes when he come up. The father thought he had a great catch, do you see. He lifted the tin off the coals, shovel and all, and he showed it to Scallon. "Look," he says, "look what my girl's at. Look what my girl's at — making tea," he says, "under the bed!"

'Scallon jumped till his feet. "Well," he says, "damn you for an old rascal. Only you're not worth it," he says, "I would bung you on your head out that door. A poor wee girl," he says, "that's going round working from early six o'clock this morning, that she couldn't do that unnoticed to you."

'Well, that settled him. He never said "tea" after it.'

Annie's 'grandma' wasn't the only female to indulge in tea-drinking on the sly as we learn from the following rhyme made about a certain Síle who was wont to make herself a brew every morning just as soon as her husband, who was not supposed to know about it, had left for his work. Síle took care always to treat her stepson to a cup or two by way of bribing him not to reveal her secret. One day, it happened that the husband was not able to go to work as usual and shortly after the boy could be heard poking a stick back and forward through a hole in the wall of the house and saying:

> *Bíonn arán agus tae ag Síle*
> *Gach uile mhaidin, gach uile mhaidin,*
> *Ní dom' dhaidí atáim dá insint*
> *Ach do pholl an bhalla, do pholl an bhalla.*[2]

> Sheila she has bread and tea
> Every morning, every morning,
> It's not my Daddy that I'm telling
> But just this hole here, just this hole here.

Chomh láidir le tae chailleach na clúide (As strong as the tea of the old hag in the corner) is a saying that might well apply to the extraordinary concoction that Kathleen Hurley of Ballymoe, County Galway, heard described in detail by an old woman (born in 1863) of the locality. Writing in 1938, she says:

'Our parents who had gone through the Famine were unaccustomed to tea. They frequently strained away the tea from the leaf. To the tea leaves they added salt, pepper and ate them with bread, using the tea as a drink. On one occasion, when I was about seven years old, I went to visit an old woman who had lived through the Famine. It was at Christmas time and she had a great welcome for us, seated us on the ground in front of the fire on the hearth and then got a small pot or skillet into which she put a naggin of water, a half pound of currants, a half pound of raisins (her supply for Christmas), a quarter pound of sugar and a handful of dried tea. She then hung the pot over the fire until it came to the boil and when it did, she broke into it a half a loaf and removing the pot from the fire and placing it on the one and only three-legged stool in the house, she gave each of us a wooden spoon to eat our feast out of the pot, including the tea leaves. We enjoyed it.'[3]

Throwing away the liquid and eating the tea leaves is a practice recorded in folk tradition from every corner of Ireland. People generally reported it as having happened in the 'next townland' or 'next parish' in an effort to distance themselves from such ill-informed antics. Other tea-drinking countries were no different from our own in this respect, however, for the virtues of the liquid as opposed to the leaf seem to have escaped the notice of other nations as well, to begin with at least, while in coffee-drinking countries it was not unknown for the coffee to be decanted and the beans eaten at one stage, just as when the potato first made its appearance in Europe, some people were said to have taken to eating the stalks and discarding the tubers.

It is clear that the arrival of the magic leaf in any community was an occasion of note, an occasion sometimes enhanced by the manner of its arrival. Such was the case in west Clare on whose jagged windswept coast a ship carrying a cargo of tea was once driven ashore. Seán Mac Mathúna of Doolin tells us about this wreck and records the lines penned by a local poet in honour of the event.

'Long ago, a ship was wrecked and ran aground on the shore at Liscannor and her crew was drowned. She was carrying a cargo of tea, an herb which the country people knew nothing about at the time. Somehow or other they managed to find out what to do with it and soon people were coming from far and wide to look for the tea. Tadhg Óg Ó Tighearna made the following verse about it:

Ní raibh aoinne as súd don Leath-Inse nó as súd go
Tír Uí Bhriocáin,
Nach raibh committee acu gach lá ina suí air dá
chrua agus dá thearra i gcorcáin;
'Dá dtagadh chugainn long eile siúicre a mbeadh
roinnt den bhiotáille ina tóin,
Dá neartódh an taoille agus an gála is go mbrisfí ina
lár an crann seoil';
Is annamh a ndineann siad guí cheart le anam na
muintire do bádh;
Ach 'Go seola Dia againn arís é mar b'anlann breá
croíúil é l' arán.'[4]

Not a soul from Lahinch to Liscannor or even to Tír
    Uí Bhriocáin,
But argued in daily committee how to brew it up,
    weak or strong;
'If only we'd a shipload of sugar with some spirits on
    board as well,
And her mast were to crack in the middle with the
    wind and the tide and the swell';
There was never a prayer for the sailors who died on
    the ship that went down,
But 'Lord, send us more of that tea soon, for no
    better sauce could be found.'

   Irish tea-drinkers of a century or more ago were not
solely dependent on occasional shipwrecks or even
smugglers for their supplies for the country was, in time,
criss-crossed by travelling tea men who peddled the product in every parish in the land. Sayings such as 'You are
as mean as a tay-man' or 'By the holy say-man, Here's
the tay-man, Open the door and let out the two dogs'
give some inkling of how unpopular they were among
the ordinary people whom they often granted liberal
credit facilities to begin with, eventually running them
into formidable debt as they became more and more

addicted to the new drink. Pilib Ó Conaill from Kilfinnane in County Limerick, writing in 1954, relates how a
local storyteller, named Dave Carey, remembered
them:

'When tea came in first and began to be drunk as a
beverage, tea men made their appearance and travelled
around selling tea. The tea men generally had one of
these high-backed cars or traps where a backed seat
went across from side to side and at the back was a
locked compartment where the tea, already weighed in
half pounds and pounds, was kept. I remember to have
seen these tea travellers myself. I've heard of some who
carried the tea in a pack at their backs and who
depended on Shank's Mare for transport.

'The tea men sometimes gave goods on credit and in
the case of our own Dave Carey, a nice little account
was run up. One fine day, Dave looked out and there
coming from the Kilfinnane direction was the tea man.
The evening before, a family of tinkers happened to be
passing and, as the night was bad, they asked leave to sit
around the kitchen fire till morning. Dave was a kind old
soul and had given them leave to do so.

'When he saw the unwelcome visitor and knowing
that a demand for prompt payment of old debts was certain, he asked the tinkers to stretch out on the floor and
pretend that they had spent the night in that fashion.
When the tea man came, he started talking about "that
bill". As he was approaching the door, Dave drew near
to him and in a whisper said, "Wait a minute, don't
come in, those inside have the bad disease and I can't
get them out. I'll go in and get your money."

'The tea man who had seen the tinkers lolling about
on the floor didn't wait to hear any more but without
another word, jumped into his vehicle and drove away
like the wind. Typhus or cholera was going round at the
time.'[5]

Marbh le tae agus marbh gan é (Killed by tea and dead without it) is a saying born of the passion with which we now dedicate ourselves to the business of drinking tea and a solid reflection of our total addiction to it, all accomplished in the space of a handful of generations. The memory of a time before tea in Ireland is fading slowly but surely, but, here and there, as we have seen, echoes from that world can still be detected. Here is one collected by Michael J. Murphy from James McKay of Layde, County Antrim in 1953:

'Old men told this passage here for the truth. It was supposed to be after the Famine or some time of scarcity anyway, and this priest, a great big man, was going round and he met these youngsters and he began to ask them what they had to eat.

'"What had you for your breakfast?" says the priest to this young lad.

'"Porridge," says the boy.

'"And what had you for your dinner?" said the priest.

'"Spuds," said the boy.

'"Well, what had you for your tea?" said the priest.

'"More spuds," said the lad.

'"And what about your supper, what had you for it?" said the priest.

'"Porridge," said the lad.

'"What about tea, did you drink no tea at all?" said the priest.

'"Do you hear the big eegit," says the boy, "and us only gets tea at Christmas!"[6]

Diarmuid Ó Crualaoich collected a couple more examples from Tadhg McCarthy, aged seventy-seven, of Maulbrack, Enniskean, County Cork in 1936. The first of these recounts the adventures of a certain 'Paddy Mickey' abroad in Cork city for the day, while the second tells of the abuse rendered to tea by Nell and

Seán, an old couple from Enniskean:

'Wisha, 'tis long ago old Paddy Mickey went to Cork of a day. There was no trains that time and, indeed, the people didn't want them either for they were well able to walk. The journey from this to Cork wasn't much for Paddy Mickey although he was old at the time.

'But, anyway, when he had his bit of business done, he felt hungry and in with him to a "cook shop". He said to the landlady that he wanted something to eat. "Very well," she says, "will you have some tea?"

'"Musha," says Paddy, "I often heard of tea and I never tasted it, but I'll try some anyway."

'Well, he wasn't long waiting when in come the land-lady with a cup of tea and bread and butter. The tea was sweetened and coloured and all. "Here," she says, "this is the best Congo tea and I hope you'll like it." Poor Paddy drank it and it tasted damned nice and when he had finished he asked for another cup. So the landlady brought him another cup, but there was no milk or sugar in this one. "Here, now," says she, "you can sweeten to your liking."

'So Paddy was looking at it — "Begor," says he, "this is like porter!"

'But, anyway, he took a good sup out of it, but if he did, it nearly roasted the mouth out of him. He got ashamed but sooner than throw it away, he drank it up. Yerra, what did the poor *amadán* know about milk or sugar!

'So when he was finished, he asked the landlady what was her charge. She told him what the charge was and, says she, "I hope you liked the tea."

'"Wisha," says Paddy, "*Grá mo chroí* the Congo tea, but may the devil sweep the "Sugar to your liking".'[7]

"Twas worse with old Nell, begor. She bought a half pound of tea from a tea man — they used to be going round the country that time, trying to sell it. Poor old Nell never saw tea before and she didn't know no more than the man in the moon how to make it and she was too proud to ask the tea man how to do it. She only pretended that she had the devil of a bargain and that she knew more about it than the tea man himself.

'She said to herself that she wouldn't touch it till Seán would come in from his work in the evening and they would have it for their supper instead of the stirabout. So she get the skillet ready, scraped and scoured it, and when the poor man came in to his supper, Nell showed him the half pound of tea, she had brought from the tea man, and said she was going to boil it for their supper.

'Well and good, she put the skillet on the fire and filled it with water and put it boiling. And when it was boiling nicely, she heeled the whole half pound of tea into it and started stirring away like the devil with the potstick. There she was, stirring and stirring, but it wasn't thickening like the stirabout.

'Poor Seán was looking at her and he starved with the hunger. "Yerra, Nell, *a ghrá*," says he, "that'll take a long time to boil, you must stir it more." He was afraid to say anything else for maybe it was a wallop of the potstick he'd get in the side of the head. So Nell kept on stirring till she was bate out and nearly roasted from the fire and Seán could hardly stand the hunger any longer and he nearly blind from watching Nell and the skillet.

'"'Tis done now, Nell, *a ghrá*, if 'twas the devil himself was in it," says he. "It should be boiled now." So Nell well proud of herself took off the skillet and poured out some of the black stuff into a basin and she was standing there looking at it a long time before she spoke. "Upon my soul, Seán," says she at last, "if the soot didn't fall into it!"

'So that's how old Nell made the tea. There wasn't much known about tea them times, boy!'[8]

The dubious reputation of the tea men soon earned them a place in the repertoire of local singers as songs began to be composed about them and their unscrupulous ways. In their hey-day, not far from the source of the River Finn in County Donegal, lived two brothers — Séamas and Peadar Breathnach (Walsh), both active observers in verse of life in Glenfinn in those days and members of the so-called school of 'Glenfinn Poets'. Some of the songs of the Walsh brothers are remembered in that area to the present day. Séamas, or Stouty, as he was also called, was spurred by the activities of a certain tea man in the area to pen what he called *Amhrán an Tae* (The Song of the Tea). His thoughts on the subject might well have been inspired by the sentiments expressed in the English proverb — 'Many estates are spent in the getting, since women for tea forsook spinning and knitting' for he had little good to say about the new vogue for drinking tea that had swept up the Finn Valley, sponsored by the merchants of Derry and Strabane. To gamble or to yield to the temptations of hard liquor was not nearly as dangerous as to succumb to the pernicious habit of drinking tea, he said, as he made his appeal to the young women of the locality, the older ones being already beyond redemption:

> *Agraím sibh, a chailíní óga, stadaí níos mó den tae,*
> *Nó beidh oraibh aithrí go fóill, má gheibh sibh cró díbh féin;*
> *Mura ndéanadh sibh ach imirt ná ól, ba deise an dóibh díbh é,*
> *Is bhéarfaidh sibh mallacht go fóill don lá thoisigh sibh a dh'ól an tae.*[9]

> Young lassies, I beseech you, make an end of drinking tea,
> For I swear that you'll regret it when married you may be;

To gamble or drink whiskey will bring you lesser
    grief,
For you'll curse the day for certain you first tasted of
    the leaf.'

Still Going Strong

The parish of Langfield in west Tyrone, like many a
rural parish in Ireland boasted, until quite recently, its
very own native distiller, a man well-known and
respected by all in the locality. Indeed, his product was
reported to be of such excellent quality that his reputation had spread far beyond the confines of his native
parish and the fruit of his labour was every bit as much
sought after as was the distiller himself by the local
police.

The police tried every trick in the book but they never
managed to catch him either in the act of making poteen
or in the act of selling and distributing it. If the police
were on the look-out, so too was he and if they were sly
and cunning then he was twice as agile and tricky. He
made regular forays into the village of Drumquin to
fetch supplies and make deliveries and his cart was
frequently searched by the local constabulary, but to no
avail. 'I have my eye on you, boy,' the sergeant told him
one day. 'In soul, sergeant, and I have my two on you,'
replied the bold distiller.

The same sergeant once received information to the
effect that his quarry was due in town with a consignment of illicit liquor concealed beneath a load of turf
and, in due course, he stepped out before your man and
halted him, cart, turf and all. Thinking to have a bit of
fun at his expense, as well as catching him red-handed

with the moonshine, the sergeant elected not to search the cart there and then, but decided instead to go through the motions of buying the load of turf from his hapless victim. The sergeant inquired how much the distiller wanted for the load of turf but he confidently replied that he already had a customer for it and that he couldn't sell it to the sergeant — much as he would like to oblige him. And so the bargaining began and continued until finally the sergeant won the day, as he thought, by offering the distiller an absolutely astronomical price, a sum of money out of all proportion to the real value of the load of turf. Reluctantly, ever so reluctantly, it seemed, our distiller yielded to the sergeant's wishes and agreed to sell. No sooner said than done — the money was swiftly paid over and the sergeant triumphantly ordered your man to steer a course with his cart for the barrack yard where he was forced without further ceremony to upend the cart and dump his load. The distiller complied with alacrity, but when the turf was dumped the police found nothing only turf and ne'er a drop of what they were really looking for. 'Twas the dear turf they had at the heel of the hunt.

Over the years, constant house raids and searches failed to turn up any of the hard evidence necessary to secure a conviction and our friend continued his merry way much to the relief of the community at large and, it was whispered, much to the relief of certain limbs of the law whom, it was said, were rather partial to a drop of your man's special brew. More enthusiastic and more scrupulous members of the force, however, spent countless days lying in the heather, spying on the lonely mountain homestead where the distiller lived and where subsequent research proved that he had actually conducted his distilling operations under the very noses of the police. But for all their spying, they never discovered anything they could pin on him.

Finally, it was decided that a plain-clothes policeman should be sent out, armed with the very best credentials and local references, in order to try and persuade this crack distiller to sell him a sample of his wares. The plain-clothes man duly arrived at the house in the heather and after the usual civilities and preliminaries, enquired if there was any chance of him coming across with a bottle or two of 'you know what'. Well, the distiller wasn't sure, but seeing as the man had come such a long way *and* that he had come so highly recommended, well, he would see what he could do. And so, the distiller, having asked his customer — the plain-clothes man — to stay put, set off up the mountain to fetch the goods from their hiding place. A short time later, he reappeared, clutching two bottles of clear liquid, one of which he proffered to the waiting customer who seized it with a howl of delight, revealed his identity and declared that now, at long last, the police had finally got their man. 'Have you, indeed?' said the wily distiller, wheeling round and dashing the second bottle, which he still held, against a nearby rock, smashing it to smithereens. 'Have you, indeed,' says he, 'well, just you taste what you have in that bottle and we'll soon see about that?' One sniff and the plain-clothes man swiftly realised that all he had for his pains was a bottle of plain ordinary water. The second bottle, so cunningly held in reserve, was, of course, the one that contained the vital evidence he so dearly wished to have.

The law also met its match on another occasion, further south, in County Cavan, as P. J. Gaynor of Bailieborough, writing in 1941, informs us. This account was given to him by Hugh McCann, a seventy-four year old shoemaker of Greaghitta, Bailieborough:

'There was a man one time by the name of Barney Ward who lived at Seeall, between Knockbride and Cootehill. He was a great poteen-maker, but the

Gauger or his men could never find out where he was making the poteen, neither could they find any of it in his possession, not, indeed, but they made many a search; but their searches were all in vain. They might as well be looking for a gold ring in a sow's lug.

'One day, a District Inspector of the police met Barney and accused him of making poteen. Barney denied it, but the District Inspector wouldn't believe him and they had a bit of an argument. "You are making it," said the District Inspector, "and I will catch you yet." Barney took up the challenge and said he, "I bet you a half sovereign that I'll bring a keg of poteen through the village of Tullyvin on Wednesday and you won't get it." The Inspector, who was a bit of a sport, took up the challenge and the wager was laid.

'The Inspector got ready and kept a posse of police in the village from 12 o'clock on the night before till 12 o'clock on Wednesday night. They searched every cart, trap and car that passed through the village. Carts containing loads of turf, hay and straw were emptied out on the road and carefully searched and examined, but not a keg of poteen could be found. Creels and *párdógs* were searched in the same way, with the same result.

'The Inspector and Barney met shortly afterwards and said the Inspector, "I won my bet."

'"No," said Barney, "but I won mine."

'"That couldn't be," said the Inspector, "for my men and myself searched every vehicle and carrier that passed through the village."

'"You didn't search everything," said Barney. "Do you remember the funeral that went past?" The Inspector said he did. "Well," said Barney, "the 'corpse' that was in the coffin was a keg of poteen."

'After the bets had been laid, Barney gathered all his friends and they agreed to march behind the coffin which contained the keg of poteen and thereby made a "funeral". The police stood to attention and gave the salute as the "funeral" was passing by. They never dreamt that the coffin contained the poteen that they were watching for.'[1]

No doubt, Barney Ward, like many another man in the trade, had to contend with spies and informers in his time. The following interesting account of what once happened to one of this breed in County Sligo was taken down in 1938 by Bríd Ní Ghamhnáin of Ballindoon, from Séamus Ó Floinn, aged sixty-five, of Drumderry, Castlebaldwin who had heard it from his mother:

'This is a story about a spy who lived in at B—— at one time and his name was C——. He was greatly hated among the people for they couldn't have a drop of poteen unnoticed to him but he hadn't the Revenue informed about it.

'One time, he found out that there was a still to be had somewhere near the Corners at Heapstown, so off he goes to Ballymote hot foot to inform the Revenue. It was during the night time that he went and he was promised five shillings of a reward if he could take the Revenue to the place where the still was before morning.

'He said that he could easily, but it was in the May-time of year and, of course, the sun rises very early on May-morning, and the old spy, it seems, didn't think about that and he was only coming along at Shralahan about a mile and a half or so from where the still was, when it was broad daylight. He began to grow very nervous, for he didn't want anyone to see him with the Revenue men so he said that he wouldn't go any further with them, that they'd be able to find the still them-selves.

'The Revenue men, of course, didn't know a thing about the place at all, or where they could find the still, so they did their best to coax him along with them for they didn't like to turn back without finding anything after coming such a distance. No coaxing, however, would make him go a step further. He just lay down before them.

'The Revenue men, when they saw that, got vexed and they started to tear the clothes off him. But it was no good — he wouldn't get up. So they took every stitch off him and they took out their knives and they cut them up as small as you wouldn't get one half inch square of cloth in the whole pile. And they'd have ripped him open only that a namesake of my own — a Sergeant Flynn — happened to be kindling his pipe along by the hedge at Shralahan and he saw them at work with the knives and he came as far as them and he told them not to do any murder.

'They then let the spy go and he had to clear in his bare pelt as far as a tailor who lived not far away. And the tailor sewed him up in sack cloth, for he wouldn't give him a decent bit of cloth and the sort of an old traitor that he was. It was the last bit of spying that he did too, for neither the Revenue nor the people had any respect for him.'[2]

Whatever about the amazing success of our Tyrone and Cavan distillers in bamboozling the law and whatever about their skills in the art of distillation, I doubt very much if even they knew how to make a run of the pure using only heather as their basic ingredient. According to Irish tradition, the secret of success in this exercise was known only to the Viking invaders, who once held sway in Ireland, and it was a secret that the Irish for all their curiosity and interest in the subject never managed to prize out of them.

The story goes that as the fortunes of the Vikings — or the Danes as they are generally called in Ireland — took a turn for the worse, it came to pass that all but two of them were slaughtered or driven into the sea by the natives.

The last two Danes — father and son, as it so happened — were on the point of being despatched by the bloodthirsty Irish when one long-headed Gael remarked that it might be a good idea to avail of the occasion to force the last of the Danes in Ireland to reveal the jealously guarded secret of the 'Heather Beer' as it was called.

At first, the two Danes refused to tell, but since they knew they were going to be killed anyway, the father eventually agreed to spill the beans, but on one condition only — namely, that the Irish should kill his son first, he being altogether too ashamed, he said, to be heard revealing the secret in front of him.

The Irish eagerly obliged by speedily disposing of the son whereupon the wise old father, secure in the knowledge that his son's tongue would never be loosed, declared that no Irishman would ever get the recipe out of him and that they could do what they liked with him, for he would never reveal the secret formula — and neither he did.

The evils of drink are well-known to all, but what made drink evil in the first place is set out for us now in the following story originally taken down in Irish in the parish of Kinvara, County Galway, in the year 1937, from a farmer who had heard it, forty years previously, from his grandfather, then aged eighty. It is called 'Noah and the Ark'.

'Long ago, when the world was about to be inundated, Noah set to make a ship for himself. No one in the world knew where he was gone or what he was doing. A man called in to his wife one day and asked her, "What is your husband doing?" said he. "I don't know," said she, "and no one in the world knows what he is doing. He has been working for a very long time and he would not tell anyone what he is doing."

'"Well, a black bear will go past here, presently," said he, "and there will be froth (*cubhar*) on him and you'll take some of the froth and put it into a drink tonight for your husband and he'll tell you everything."

'When Noah came home at night and ate his supper, his wife said, "Perhaps you would take a drink?"

'"I shall," said Noah. She put the froth on the drink and gave it to him and he told her everything he was doing.

'He went to his work on the following day. The first blow he made was heard throughout the world and everyone knew what he was doing then. When he had the ship ready he launched it, taking his wife and children and everything with him — even the dog. The dog had no room and its nose was out and that is what left its nose cold ever since.

'The devil came to Noah's daughter and said to her: "You should take me with you."

'"How could I take you?" said the girl.

'"Oh, I'll turn myself into a brooch," said he, "and you'll put me in your blouse and I'll go in that manner."

'"That will do then," said she.

'When the vessel was afloat, she began to sink and Noah did not know why it was sinking. He had a bottle of holy water and he went round the vessel sprinkling it on everything. A drop of the holy water fell on the brooch. The brooch went from the girl in a flame and the vessel rose again and proceeded on its way safe and sound.

'It was the devil who came to Noah's wife and told her to put the froth on the drink. That is what has made drink evil ever since.'[3]

There is an Irish saying which specifies three things every true tippler should know how to handle when it comes to drink — *é a ól, é a íoc agus é a iompar* (how to drink it, how to pay for it and how to carry it). In 1930, Éamonn Furlong, aged eighty-one, from Duncormack, County Wexford, recalled for the benefit of Domhnall de Buitléar the trouble that the inability to cope with the last of these three stipulations once landed a fellow Wexfordman by the name of Paddy Mullowney in, a spot of bother which, in its turn, nearly resulted in a certain Paddy Delaney ending his days at the end of a rope. Here's what happened:

'This is a song that was composed by a local poet — or supposed to be at any rate — about an inquest that was held over a man named Paddy Mullowney. He got drunk and he hurt himself and he was given up for dead. He wasn't really dead at all, but the inquest went on, nevertheless, and this song was composed about him.

'Twas Paddy Mullowney so jolly and frisky,
Went into a shebeen to get his sack full,
But tumbled out again, well dosed with ould whiskey,
As silly as an ass and as drunk as a fool.

But a bit of an accident met with our rover,
Who struck the wall's edge with the side of his head,
And the lid of a coal box he just tumbled over,
And he fancied the while he was just going to bed.

Some friends passing by hauled him out of the river,
And sent for a doctor his sickness to cure,
And swore that poor Pat was a bad Billy diver,
As now he lay dead as a nail in a dure.

They gathered the old local jury to try him,
But Pat not half liking them, like his ould wife,
Kept groaning and grunting the while they stood
    round him,
And came, when it suited him, right back to life.

"Arra, fellas, *a ghrá,* will you give over your teasing,
I'm as lively as a bee and am able to say boo,"

"Be quiet you ould *scraiste* and keep your tongue aisy
Do you imagine but the doctor knows better than
   you?"

So the jury went on with the case without bother,
And questioned the doctor about his belief,
They said poor Delaney was guilty of murder,
And vowed that they'd hang him in spite of his grief.

'Delaney wasn't hanged however, but he was saved
through his own cuteness. They decided to hang him all
right and at that time, in probable cases, they used to
decide it this way. They would get two slips of paper and
on one they'd write "life" and on the other they'd write
"death". They would then place these two slips of paper
in a hat and they'd blindfold the prisoner and then he
would draw one of these slips of paper from the hat and
if he pulled the one with "life" written on it then he was
let live but if he drew the one with "death" written on it,
he was hanged.

'However, they had something terrible against this
poor unfortunate devil so they put the two slips of paper
into the hat and "death" was written on each of them.
Paddy got wind of this beforehand so he used his ould
head when the time came. He was blindfolded and the
hat was placed before him and he put his hand down in
the hat and drew up one of the slips of paper and tore it
up quickly into a thousand parts before anyone could
find out what was written on it and then he said, "Look
at the slip in the hat and if "life" is written on it I am
satisfied to be hanged, but if "death" is written on it I am
to be left alive". So they took the slip from the hat and
they found that "death " was written on it and so Paddy
was let live.'[4]

Finally, another story about a famous poteen-maker
who lived in a certain part of Ireland which shall be
nameless. He was well-known for the excellent quality

of his product and equally well for an abundant ready supply of it. Disaster struck, however, when one of the old-time missioners descended upon the locality to preach against drink and especially against producers and purveyors of illicit spirits. Every man, woman and child in the district was ordered to deliver up every single vessel or object that had ever come into contact with poteen, whether it be stills and worms, or jars and eggstands (eggcups) — the latter being the customary measure in which poteen was served in that part of the world. Not only that, and God knows that was bad enough, but making, tasting or handling the stuff in any way was declared a sin to be confessed to the missioner before the week was out and, as you might well understand, this injunction placed our talented distiller in a rather embarrassing position.

The days of the mission went by one by one and the pile of receptacles of all shapes and sizes, not to mention the display of distilling apparatus of various vintages and stages of operational usefulness, grew higher and higher outside the parish church in readiness for the grand bonfire which was to be lit on the closing night of the mission, a conflagration designed to crown the ardent missioner's efforts at rendering this community more sober than it had ever been before.

The close of the mission was drawing ever nearer and the champion of the district had still to bear his breast to the missioner whose strictures on the hard stuff grew ever harsher from day to day and whose warnings to those who had not as yet confessed to making or even drinking it grew ever more dire.

At last our hero yielded and set off for the church to make his confession. Hard by the church there was a house with a squad of young children in it and before facing the music, the reluctant penitent entered this house and politely asked the woman of the house to kindly remove her infant child from the cradle so that he could get into it. This rather odd request was, perhaps, not as outlandish as it may sound to modern ears for old time wooden cradles were sturdy affairs and usually of not inconsiderable bulk. The good woman did as she was bid and your man settled himself into the cradle beside the fire. "Rock me, now," says he to the woman of the house. So, she rocked him a bit and after a while he stepped out of the cradle and thanked her kindly for her civility and her patience with him. He took his leave of her and proceeded straight into the nearby church. No sooner had he entered the confession box than the eager missioner immediately raised the subject of poteen, its distillation and drinking, demanding to know if he had ever had anything to do with it in any shape or form.

"'Well, now, father," said your man, "to tell you the God's honest truth, I can safely say that I have neither touched, tasted, seen nor smelt that stuff since I was rocked in the cradle!'"

Sláinte!

Niall Ó Dubhthaigh died on 29 May 1961, at the ripe old age of eighty-seven. His name is not a household name in Ireland though it certainly should be, for he was one of the greatest *seanchaí*s of his day and his capacity for certain kinds of lore has rarely been surpassed, as those familiar with it will readily agree. Two articles published in *Béaloideas,* the Journal of the Folklore of Ireland Society — *Buailteachas i dTír Chonaill*[1] (Booleying in Donegal), a marvellously detailed account of the ancient custom of transhumance, as practised in Donegal, in days gone by, and another article *Laethe na Seachtaine*[2] containing a mass of information connected with the days of the week, is all that has appeared in print of his vast store of knowledge of traditional things. They represent only the tip of the iceberg, for full-time folklore collector Seán Ó hEochaidh spent more than three years coming and going in his company and, in that time, managed to cover with him the vast amount of ground contained between the covers of Seán Ó Súilleabháin's *Handbook of Irish Folklore*. There was hardly a question in its 699 pages that Niall Ó Dubhthaigh wasn't able to respond to and the evidence of his virtuosity in this field is there for all to see in the many thousands of manuscript pages of folk tradition which Seán Ó hEochaidh took down from him.

Here, in translation, is what Seán Ó hEochaidh had to say of this great *seanchaí*.

'Niall was a special person possessed of unusual qualities. He had all the gentleness of the old people in him and he had a great sense of humour but at the same time he could be as serious as any man in the twinkling of an eye. He was remarkably observant and very patient but, above everything else, he had an extraordinary memory. On top of that he had a superb command of his native Irish and of English too, enough to astound the many scholars and others from every part of Europe that met up with him through me. They said they had never met anything to equal him.'[3]

Let us join Niall Ó Dubhthaigh and Seán Ó hEochaidh now at the point in their conversations where the talk had turned to drink and, in particular, the business of drinking traditional toasts.[4]

'In my young days, when two or three men went in for a drink together, it was the custom for them to go into a back room — a snug. They never stood at the counter. Each of them would be carrying an ash plant and one of them would strike three hefty blows on the table and, in a flash, the barmaid would be in to see what they wanted. She would be ordered to bring them a half-pint of whiskey and, in due course, she would return with a jug and a glass. Should there be ten men in the company, they would still only have the one glass. The man who had ordered and paid for the drink would then stand up and hand a glass of whiskey to the man nearest to him, who would then say — "Here's health" (*Seo do shláinte*) to which the first man might answer, "God grant you health" (*Sláinte ó Dhia duit*). That's the kind of toast they used to drink and it was always with a blow of the ash plant that they summoned the barman or barmaid.

'Long ago, when poteen was plentiful and whiskey was cheap, there would be drink at every *meitheal*. The men didn't get paid, but at least they got a good drink. They used to drink toasts on such occasions too and the man might raise his glass like this — "Good health boys, one and all, and may God bless you and the work." (*Bhur sláinte uilig go léir, a bhuachaillí, agus go gcuirí Dia rath oraibh féin agus ar bhur gcuid oibre*).'

Niall Ó Dubhthaigh went on to describe what he called *Móide Fhear na Tearmann* (The Termon-man's Pledge):

'There was a man in Termon one time that was very much given to the drop. The clergy were constantly after him to give up the drink but found him absolutely impossible to deal with. One day, he met the priest and the priest gave him such a severe dressing down that he finally agreed to give up the bottle — on condition that he would continue to be allowed to sample an odd wee drop now and then, the "now and then" being as he said, *Ag bainis agus ag baisteadh, Cuid mhónadh Mhac Cais-*

leáin, Dhá ghloine sa lá, Agus talamh an Bhearnais saor.
(At weddings and christenings, at Mac Caisleáin's turf
(*meitheal*), Two glasses a day, And Barnes to be
exempt).'

In other words, the Termon-man would agree to
giving it up, if he was rationed to two glasses a day and
was allowed to drink at weddings and christenings. The
significance of his other two *caveats* lies in the fact that
Mac Caisleáin was renowned for the generosity with
which he dispensed liquor at his annual turf *meitheal*
while Barnes was the location of a noted shebeen in the
area. Some pledge, indeed!

The Termon-man might well have included funerals
in his pledge too, as Niall Ó Dubhthaigh explains:

'They'd have a few drinks at funerals too. After the
burial, friends and neighbours would gather together
with the bereaved family in a pub and would be treated
by them to a drink. They had toasts specially suited for
the occasion. The deceased would be praised to the sky
and everyone who had a drink would raise his glass and
say — Eternal rest to the soul that has joined the host of
the dead. (*Sólás síorraí don anam a chuaigh ar shlua na
marbh*).'

Matchmaking was also an operation for the smooth
execution of which liberal doses of whiskey were considered necessary —

'They used to bring a couple of gallons of whiskey
with them in a little three-gallon keg. Naturally enough,
the publican would be very pleased at having sold that
much whiskey to them and he might join them for a
drink or two himself. They would raise their glasses and
he would say — "Good health and good luck and may
your journey be successful and may the Lord spare the
man that's going to settle down from heartbreak, harm
and want. (*Seo bhur sláinte, go gcuirí Dia an t-ádh
oraibh, agus go n-éirí bhur dturas libh, agus go sábhálaí*

Dia an fear atá ag gabháil i gceann an tsaoil ar chrá croí, díth nó díobháil)."

'They would go to the house then and knock at the door and ask if the young woman in question was at home. They would know immediately if they were welcome or not, but whether they were or not, they would pass round the whiskey, anyway, always making sure that the old couple in the house got a drink. Then the talk would start about the dowry and all that. Sometimes, in the end, they might be successful. Often they were refused and more often again it happened that when the father and mother had agreed to the match, the girl left the kitchen, went up to her room and made off out the window. That happened a hundred times in this place!

'She might have another fellow and it would be a runaway marriage and her parents wouldn't know a thing about it till this fellow would arrive at the house with whiskey. Whether there'd be a welcome or not for him at the time, they'd drink his whiskey, anyway, and when they had drunk their fill of it, that's when they might begin to fall out about the runaway marriage. But, after a couple of days, they'd soon get over that and it would be a pity of anyone that would come between them!'

Sometimes, when a girl was allowed to pick and choose herself, things didn't work out quite as she expected —

'I heard tell of a girl round here one time who was in love with two boys — or, rather, the two boys were head over heels in love with her. She was very keen on one of them, but she didn't think much of the other, in fact, as far as he was concerned, she didn't really care whether she saw him or not. The fellow that only made an appearance now and then was the one she liked best, but the other boy whom she didn't fancy so much had a habit of turning up every other night.

'One night, the two of them landed together and this is the toast that she drank to them and the welcome she bid them both:

> Here's the health of "Comes often",
> And here's the health of "Comes seldom",
> More's the pity that "Comes seldom" only comes
> Half as often as "Comes often".

> *(Seo sláinte mhinic-a-thig,*
> *Agus seo sláinte mhinic-nach-dtig,*
> *Is trua nach dtig minic-nach-dtig,*
> *Leath comh minic le minic-a-thig.)*

Sometimes a girl was left on the shelf, or nearly left on the shelf, as was the case with Róise Ní Chailleoige's daughter, Sorcha — approaching forty and no offers. In an anecdote called *Sláinte Róise Ní Chailleoige* (Róise Ní Chailleoige's Toast) Niall Ó Dubhthaigh describes how this anxious mother couldn't contain herself with joy when things took a sudden and unexpected turn for the better.

'Róise had a neighbour, a man called Micí, a widower who had been left with two small children. Micí decided to look for a wife and one night he headed over to Róise Ní Chailleoige to ask for her daughter's hand in marriage. Needless to say, Róise was only too pleased to have the opportunity of getting poor Sorcha off her hands at long last and when Micí handed her a glass of whiskey, she blurted out —

'"Welcome," said she, "and good health. You have a grand farm of land and it's here you were born and raised. 'Tis long we've waited for you and, God bless you, you have a good wife away with you! *(Sé do bheatha, a deir sí, agus seo do shláinte. Tá farm maith talaimh agat agus tógadh ar an bhaile thú. Is fada muid ag fanacht leat agus go gcuirí Dia rath ort, tá bean mhaith*

117

toighe leat!)"'

Like many a Donegalman before and after him, Niall
Ó Dubhthaigh spent a good many years living and working in Scotland. He recalls those days —

'I remember years ago in Scotland, when a crowd of
boys from this place would be drinking together, it's
many the funny toast that would be proposed. This is
one toast that the Donegalmen always drank when they
got together —

Here's to the hand that made the ball,
That shot Lord Leitrim in Donegal!

'I heard another one too that used to really annoy the
Connachtmen that were working there —

Here's the health of all Ireland—except County
Mayo,
And whoever doesn't like that knows where he can go!

(*Seo sláinte na hÉireann ach Contae Mhaigh Eo,
Is an té nach maith leis sin nach raibh sé i bhfad
beo!*).'

Here, the unconventional use of *ach* rather than *agus,*
'but' rather than 'and', turned the normal versions of
this fairly common toast on its head and was sufficient to
drive the Connachtmen to fury and, no doubt, instigate
many a bout of fisticuffs between them and their
neighbours to the north across the waters of Donegal
Bay.

'The Mayo people themselves could be pretty
sanguine about the fate of their own fellow citizens, as is
clear from the following toast taken down in that very
county:

The health of all Ireland and of County Mayo,
And when that much is dead, may we still be on the
go;
From the County of Meath, the health of the hag,

Not of her but her drink is the reason we brag;
Your health one and all, from one wall to the other,
And, you outside there — speak up, brother!

(Sláinte na hÉireann agus Chontae Mhaigh Eo,
Agus nuair a chailltear an méid sin, go raibh muide
*   beo;*
Sláinte na caillí a bhí i gContae na Mí,
Agus ní le grá don gcaillí ach le grá don bhraon;
Bhur sláinte ó bhalla go balla,
Agus an té atá sna doirse dúinte, labhraidís!)[5]

'"No nonsense" is the keynote of another toast from
Achill Island in the same county:

The health of the salmon and of the trout,
That swim back and forward near the Bull's Mouth;
Don't ask for saucepan, jug or mug,
Down the hatch — drink it up!

(Seo sláinte an bhric is an bhradáin,
A chuaigh siar is aniar ag Béal an Bhulláin;
Ná hiarr jug, mug nó sáspan,
Ach seo siar an píobán!)[6]

It is predominantly Irish-language toasts that have
been noted here hitherto and, perhaps, it is time to turn
our attention to some toasts collected in the English
language in Ireland.

Michael J. Murphy, during his sojourn in the Sperrin
Mountains in County Tyrone as full-time collector for
the former Irish Folklore Commission was fortunate to
come across the following examples. First of all, one
with historical, not to mention political, overtones:

Here's to the pigeon of the green wing,
A Roman priest and a Fenian king,
Here's to King William —
With a knife in his heart and a fork in his liver,

That he may never die or no one kill him,
Till he goes to hell and the devil gets 'melling' him![7]

Quite a few of these Tyrone toasts have what you
might call a 'fire and brimstone' flavour. Take this salu-
tation, for example, said to have been pronounced by a
man who went seeking a wife:

Here's from the roof rib to the foundation stone,
All sorts of bother and misfortune,
Hell's blazes and damnation to any man who has a
    daughter —
And won't give her to me![8]

'Here's that we may never see hell, jail or the
poorhouse' was also a common enough saying, milder in
sentiment than either the previous or the following
announcement:

Here's health and prosperity,
To you and all your posterity,
And them that doesn't drink with sincerity,
That they may be damned for all eternity![9]

Words of equally ferocious intent occur in a toast which
I collected a few years ago from the late Thomas Burns
(Tommy Bhess) of Portacloy, County Mayo:

Long, long ago, in Queen Anne's time,
When a Catholic might lose his head,
Dan, in his prime, said, 'That's a crime —
For when taking a tot, let Sasanach or Scot,
Drink a toast, or else,' said he,
'On the crown of their head,
With their arse in the air,
It's in hell that they shall be.'

(*Bhí an t-am sin ann le linn Queen Anne,*
Go mbainthí an ceann de Chaitliceach,
Ach, d'éirigh Dan agus chraith sé a cheann,
'Albanach nó Sasanach,' a dúirt sé,

'*Nach n-ólfadh linne a shláinte,*
Mullach a chinn in Ifreann,
Agus poll a thóna in airde!')

Most toasts, however, were much less malicious in character than these and were more often designed to raise a laugh than to poke fun or score political points. Especially suited for this purpose were toasts in the form of tongue twisters which were always popular, no doubt because it was doubly difficult to say them while 'under the influence'. Take the following, for example:

Here's to you as good as you are,
And to me as bad as I am;
I'm as good as you are,
Bad and all as I am.[10]

and

Here's to you and yours and to mine and ours,
And if mine and ours ever come across you and
yours,
I hope you and yours will do as much for mine and
ours,
As mine and ours done for you and yours![11]

Many of our Irish drinking toasts, especially those in the Irish language, have a real medieval feel about them. They frequently combine, in a frank and simple way, heartfelt pious sentiments with an equally heartfelt intent to imbibe, putting puritanical attitudes towards drink to shame in the process. The ordinary everyday 'Good Luck', 'Good Health' or 'Here's Fortune' seem very curt and colourless by comparison with their elegant spirituality. What could be purer of purpose than the prayerful toast I once heard pronounced in the Blue Stack Mountains in County Donegal — *Sláinte na glóire gile duit* (The health of bright glory to you) or what surpasses the fervour of this toast from County

Cork — *Seo é an tArd-Mhac do leath a ghéaga ar an gcrois dá chéasadh, Agus sláinte na mná rug mac gan chéile, Agus sláinte Naomh Pádraig do bheannaigh Éire*[12] (Here's to the High Son who stretched his limbs for crucifixion on the cross, And here's the health of the Virgin Mother, And here's the health of St Patrick who blessed Ireland).

Notes

IFC = Irish Folklore Collection — the folklore manuscript collection incorporating the holdings of the former Irish Folklore Commission now housed at the Department of Irish Folklore, University College, Dublin.

THE WILD RAPPAREE
1. As quoted in the *Ulster Journal of Archaeology,* Vol. V (1857), pp. 255-256.
2. As quoted in the *Ulster Journal of Archaeology,* Vol. VII (1859), p. 76.
3. *Dublin University Magazine,* January 1847, p. 43.
4. Cf. *Dublin University Magazine,* January 1847, p. 43-50.
5. Tape-recording deposited in Sound Archive, Department of Irish Folklore, University College, Dublin.
6. *The Shamrock,* Vol. 12 (1875), pp. 517-518.
7. Cf. *Journal of the Cork Historical and Archaeological Society,* Vol. XI (1905), pp. 67-71.
8. Cf. *The Dublin Saturday Magazine,* Vol. II (1865-1867), pp. 483-484.
9. Cf. *Journal of the Kildare Archaeological Society,* Vol IV (1903-1905), pp. 348-349.
10. Cf. IFC Ms. Vol. 407, pp. 181-192 *passim.*

HAGS AND HARES
1. Seán Ó Súilleabháin, *A Handbook of Irish Folklore* (Dublin 1942 & Detroit 1970).
2. Ó Súilleabháin, *op. cit.* pp. 180-181, 388-389.
3. Cf. *Béaloideas* (The Journal of the Folklore of Ireland Society), Vol. III (1931-1932), pp. 331-332.
4. IFC Ms. Vol. 1010, pp. 182-184. The original Irish text is printed in *Béaloideas* Vols. 45-47 (1977-1979), pp. 112-113.
5. IFC Ms. Vol. 744, pp. 440-446.

THE DAY OF THE HORSE
1. For a comprehensive survey of the horse in Irish folk tradition, cf. 'An Capall i mBéaloideas na hÉireann' by Daithí Ó hÓgáin in *Béaloideas,* Vols. 45-47 (1977-1979), pp. 199-243.
2. Cf. IFC MS. Vol. 117, pp. 40-42.
3. Cf. IFC Sms. Vol. 686, pp. 113-114.
4. Cf. IFC MS. Vol. 656, pp. 81.
5. Cf. IFC Sms. Vol. 353, p. 570.
6. IFC MS. Vol. 1245, pp. 354-373.

CATS
1. IFC MS. Vol. 406, pp. 19-20.
2. IFC MS. Vol. 1403, p. 462.
3. IFC MS. Vol. 404, pp. 158-164.
4. Patrick Kennedy, *The Fireside Stories of Ireland* (Dublin 1870), pp. 149-150.

FIRST AND LAST
1. IFC MS. Vol. 389, pp. 198-200.

2. IFC MS. Vol. 278, pp. 304-322.
3. IFC MS. Vol. 1118, pp. 273-274.

DEAD AND BURIED
1. IFC MS. Vol. 1470, pp. 22-23.
2. Cf. *Béaloideas*, Vol. VI (1936), pp. 260-261.
3. *Béaloideas*, Vol. XII (1942), pp. 186-187.
4. T. Crofton Croker, *Fairy Legends and Traditions of the South of Ireland* (London 1828), pp. 21-27.

BEGGING THEIR BIT
1. IFC MS. Vol. 1403, pp. 78-80.
2. IFC MS. Vol. 463, pp. 13-14.
3. IFC MS. Vol. 84, p. 322.
4. IFC MS. Vol. 389, pp. 247-250.
5. IFC MS. Vol. 616, p. 319.
6. IFC MS. Vol. 1834, pp. 3-5.
7. IFC MS. Vol. 1344, pp. 370-373.
8. IFC MS. Vol. 1014, pp. 361-364.
9. IFC MS. Vol. 1014, p. 313.

TEA
1. IFC MS. Vol. 1242, pp. 581-82.
2. *Irisleabhar na Gaeilge*, Vol. XI, July 1901, p. 116.
3. IFC MS. Vol. 463, p. 140.
4. IFC MS. Vol. 41, pp. 209-210.
5. IFC MS. Vol. 1380, pp. 24-27.
6. IFC MS. Vol. 1360, p. 94.
7. IFC MS. Vol. 203, pp. 491-493.
8. IFC MS. Vol. 203, pp. 493-495.
9. *Irisleabhar na Gaeilge*, Vol. VIII, November 1897, pp. 118-119.

STILL GOING STRONG
1. IFC MS. Vol. 791, pp. 438-440.
2. IFC MS. Vol. 463, pp. 74-75.
3. IFC MS. Vol. 349, p. 153.
4. IFC MS. Vol. 220, pp. 147-149.

SLÁINTE
1. *Béaloideas*, Vol. XIII (1943), pp. 130-158.
2. *Béaloideas*, Vol. XVII (1947), pp. 131-174.
3. *Béaloideas*, Vol. XXVIII (1960 [1962]), p. 136.
4. IFC MS. Vol. 800, pp. 134-163 *passim*.
5. IFC MS. Vol. 79, pp. 328.
6. IFC MS. Vol. 79, p. 623.
7. IFC MS. Vol. 1215, p. 474.
8. IFC MS. Vol. 1218, p. 325.
9. IFC MS. Vol. 1215, p. 199.
10. IFC MS. Vol. 1215, p. 196.
11. IFC MS. Vol. 1218, p. 179.
12. IFC MS. Vol. 54, p. 406.

LONG AGO BY SHANNON SIDE
Edmund Lenihan

Long Ago by Shannon Side is a heart-warming collection of colourful folktales and stories which were
told around the turf fire in days gone by. There are
stories about buried treasure, haunted places and
strange meetings with the 'Good People'. We read
about reactionary landlords, idiosyncratic priests
and meet a host of local characters. Above all we
see the people of Ireland at work and at play, in
sorrow and in joy.

As every generation dies out part of their way of
life dies with them. Already there is a whole generation of adults who have never enjoyed sitting by
an open hearth in a thatched cottage listening to
the old people remembering the way they used to
live.

Jimmy Armstrong, whose tales these are, possesses
the gift of storytelling usually associated with the
seanchaithe of long ago and his stories are guaranteed to entertain the reader.

THE BEDSIDE BOOK OF IRISH FABLES AND LEGENDS

Maureen Donegan

In this fascinating book of Irish legends the reader will meet many old friends from Ireland's distant past. Head and shoulders above them all is Cuchulainn, whose birth was surrounded with mystery and whose life was full of battles and love, enchantment and treachery. Maureen Donegan traces his career from the precocious child through his lusty youth to the proud middle-aged, battled-scarred hero.

We also meet the Lupracans, the miniature water sprites who live under the sea, Fergus and the Monster, Fionn and the Gilla Dacker and discover how Diarmuid got his Love Spot. We see them struggling with life, sometimes helped by a bit of magic but as often hindered by it. They may be larger than life but they are overwhelmingly and endearingly human.

THE BEDSIDE BOOK OF THE WEST OF IRELAND
Padraic O'Farrell

This is a book which will remind you of those things about the west of Ireland that you would like to remember and read over and over again.

The west of Ireland has always had a particular fascination for the native Irish and visitor alike. Its mountains, valleys, rivers, lakes and seaboard boast a visual and intellectual beauty unrivalled by any other part of Ireland — every acre echoes a legend and every stone a piece of history.

The Bedside Book of the West of Ireland takes its reader on a nostalgic journey by re-introducing us to some much loved pieces such as 'The Men of the West', 'The Boys form the County Mayo', 'Clonmacnoise', 'The Dog of Aughrim', 'Mary of Meelick', 'Westport Town', 'Lament of Mac Liag for Kincora' and 'The West's Asleep'. Padraic O'Farrell quotes some extracts from *The Book of Ballymote, The Adventures of Donnchadh Ruadh Mac Con-Mara,* Hardiman's *History of Galway* and Mr. and Mrs. C. S. Hall's *The West and Connemara* and he also gives us some fascinating information about Cormac Mac Airt, Michael Davitt, Captain Boycott and a host of other people.

The Bedside Book of the West of Ireland could truthfully be classified as a book to be taken and cherished if one had to live on a desert island.

SOME STRANGE EXPERIENCES OF
KITTY THE HARE
Victor O' D. Power.

Hundreds of thousands of people all over Ireland were entertained and thrilled in their youth by reading the homely and racy adventures of Kitty the Hare in magazines and journals. Kitty was the famous travelling woman of Ireland and according to her 'you'll find good, hospitable people everywhere you go in Ireland.....I'm after travelling through Munster....and through most of Leinster and some of Connaught and part of Ulster as well faith, so I know what I'm talking about....'

Here, for the first time, we have collected some of the best and most exciting of these stories and so as Kitty says, 'Let ye all gather close to me, and stir up the turf into a blaze, the way you'll have some sort of courage, Mossa, to listen to my tale...'

SUPERSTITIONS OF THE IRISH COUNTRY PEOPLE
Padraic O'Farrell

Do you know why it is considered unlucky

— to meet a barefooted man?
— to start out on a journey on the tenth of November?
— to get married on a Saturday?

Irish country people believed that fairies were always present among them and that around the next corner or in the very next clump of thistles there might well be somebody lurking, who would lead them to the crock of gold at the end of the rainbow. Fairies were good to mortals who observed the superstitions which called for leaving them food, not throwing out water without shouting a warning to them and so on. They even parted with some of their golden apples, waters of wisdom and swords of knowledge to such considerate people.

In the Irish countryside life still has dignity and people are not mere statistics. Going to work, to sea, to weddings and to wakes — at all of these there were fascinating customs to be observed.

THE IRISH BEDSIDE BOOK
Edited by John M. Feehan.

This is a book which will remind you of those things about Ireland that you would like to remember and read over and over again. In these pages you can let your mind wander in lazy reflection through song, story, poem, speech and anecdote with a delightful blend of inspiration, consolation and laughter.

At the end of a tiring day what better way to guide the weary eyes to sleep than with a soothing thought from the mind of some Irish writer still living, or dead a thousand years.

But *The Irish Bedside Book* is not only a bed-time reader, it is also a friend on journeys by land, sea or air — an inseparable companion for all those who love Ireland. It is a book that could truthfully be classified as one to be taken and cherished if one had to live alone on a desert island.

www.ingramcontent.com/pod-product-compliance
Ingram Content Group UK Ltd.
Pitfield, Milton Keynes, MK11 3LW, UK
UKHW030622070125
453151UK00009B/237

9 781781 179147